Namtar – The Bram Stoker Journals

C.D. Jones

First Edition: April 2026

ebook ISBN: 979-8-9937130-0-7

Paperback: 979-8-9937130-1-4

Audiobook: 979-8-9937130-2-1 (Stay Tuned)

Published by:

Lopsco Publishing LLC, P. O. Box 686, McMinnville, TN 37111

Printed in the United States of America

Contents

Should anyone find this after my death —

These are my private notes. Research, I held close. Research for the novel and what I told my wife Florence—-that was not entirely true.

What follows must seem like the ravings of a Gothic novelist too immersed in his own fiction. I wish that were so.

I was commissioned to write a lie. This journal contains the truth I buried.

The Duke assured me that these documents would be destroyed after my death. If you are reading this, either he failed, or someone decided the truth matters more than the comfortable fiction I helped create.

Judge for yourself.

—Abraham Stoker

Abraham Stoker

August 1887

Weston Family Crest

1887

Late August, 1887

Somewhere in the Carpathian Mountains Region

Cannot think clearly. Hands still shaking. Record it while fresh. While I can still write.

The train had to detour—some issue with the tracks ahead, the conductor said in broken German. We stopped at a station I didn't recognize, nowhere near my intended destination. The name of the place escaped me in the confusion of languages and my own exhaustion. I only knew I needed rest.

I found lodging at a nearby coaching inn. Basic accommodations, but the innkeeper seemed honest enough, if anxious about something. After securing my room, I should have retired for the evening. But the night was still young, and I've always been restless in unfamiliar places.

I headed out after dark. Walked right into it. All happened so quickly.

The village—

The screams—

The thing in the darkness—

No. Facts. Just facts.

Start again.

What I saw tonight. My hand shakes even now, hours later, safe in this coaching inn. The village—God help me, the screams. The thing that moved through the darkness was no wolf, no bear, nothing natural.

And the men who fought it. Led by an English nobleman—a Duke, by his bearing—who moved with military precision. They had silver weapons. Strange devices that glowed with unnatural light. They killed it, finally, though three of their number fell in the attempt.

The Duke saw me watching from where I'd hidden. Our eyes met across the carnage. He knows I saw.

But he let me go with only these words: "Forget what you witnessed here, Mr. Stoker. For your own sake." But how can I forget? How can anyone forget such horror?

And – he knew my name. How did this duke know my name?

1888

January, 1888

London

A curious summons arrived this morning by private messenger—not the common post, mind, but a liveried man who waited whilst I read the letter and insisted upon a verbal reply to carry back to his master. The seal bore a crest I did not recognize, though it spoke of old lineage: twin moons above a shield.

The letter itself was brief, almost curt in its formality, yet the request it contained has occupied my thoughts the whole of the day. His Grace, Edmund Weston, Duke of Weston, requests my presence at Weston Hall in Sussex to discuss "a matter of some delicacy touching upon historical research." Why would a duke concern himself with a theatre manager who pens sensational tales in what spare hours the Lyceum allows? Irving released me from tomorrow's rehearsals when I showed him the letter—he knows the nobility must be indulged—but I confess the whole business strikes me as decidedly odd.

I gave the messenger my reply: I would come on the 23rd, if that date proved convenient to His Grace.

Florence thinks it a fine opportunity, though she knows as little as I what the Duke might want. Perhaps some family history he wishes dramatized? Or old legends from Sussex he believes might furnish material for my writing?

I shall discover soon enough. Yet there is something in the tone of that letter—a weight beneath the courtesy—that gives me pause. He writes of more than historical curiosities – as though they are necessity.

***

12th March, 1888

Weston Hall, Sussex

Cannot sleep. The specimen—grey skin, black eyes, teeth like needles. Duke says twelve dead at Whitby, '85. Wants me to write about it. Fiction. To hide truth.

Impossible. Yet I saw it.

I am not a man easily unsettled. Years of illness in childhood, followed by the peculiar education of managing artists and their temperaments, have given me what I believe to be steady nerves. Yet tonight, as I sit in the guest chambers of Weston Hall with a fire burning low in the grate, I find my hand unsteady as I write.

The approach to the estate was like traveling backward through England's history. Ancient oaks—surely predating the Tudors—formed a canopy so dense the afternoon sun scarce penetrated. The Hall itself rises from the Sussex countryside as if it had grown there, stone by stone, across centuries. Grand, yes, but weathered as old parchment, bearing the marks of every storm England has endured since William landed at Pevensey.

His Grace met me at the door himself. No butler, no ceremony—simply the Duke of Weston, a man perhaps three-score years, tall and spare, with the bearing of a soldier despite his exalted rank. His handshake was firm, his eyes sharp and assessing in a manner that put me more in mind of a military commander than a peer of the realm.

"Mr. Stoker," he said, "you are punctual. I appreciate that in a man. Come—we've much to discuss, and precious little time for pleasantries."

He led me not to a drawing room, as I had anticipated, but deeper into the Hall. The architecture changed as we walked—paneled Tudor giving way to older stone, the passages growing narrower, the air cooler. We descended stairs I am certain date to the Norman period, perhaps to the very founding of the house in 1066. At last we entered a chamber that must form part of the original foundation, lit by oil lamps that cast shadows dancing across walls of unmortared stone.

"My family has occupied this land for eight hundred and twenty-two years," His Grace said, his voice echoing slightly in that ancient space. "These walls have kept many secrets, Mr. Stoker. Tonight I am going to share one with you. What I show you must never appear in print as fact. But I need you to write it nonetheless—disguised as fiction."

What he revealed in that vault beneath Weston Hall—I struggle to find adequate words, though words are my profession. The thing preserved there in spirits looked almost human. Almost. But the proportions were wrong, the angles of bone beneath grey-pallored skin too sharp, the teeth filed or grown to points, and the eyes—even in death, even clouded by preservation—black as a moonless night and somehow *wrong* in a way that made my skin crawl.

"This creature," he said, his voice flat with the tone of a man relating facts he has long since ceased to feel emotion about, "killed twelve people near Whitby in the summer of 1885. We contained it before more lives were lost, but not before the local newspapers began speaking of vampires. The stories are spreading faster than we can contain them, Mr. Stoker. People are asking questions. Seeking answers. And the truth—" he gestured at the thing in the jar, "—is too dangerous for them to know."

He poured brandy then—French, older than I am by the taste—and laid before me a proposition as extraordinary as the preserved creature. He wishes me to write a novel. Not merely any novel, but a sensation about vampires that will give the public a fiction so compelling, so thoroughly detailed, that it will supplant the truth they are stumbling toward.

"Make them romantic," His Grace instructed. "Aristocratic. Seductive. Give them rules—garlic, crosses, sunlight. Create a vampire that *cannot* exist in nature, one so removed from reality that the very word 'vampire' will conjure your fiction rather than," again that gesture toward the jar—"the truth. We need people to believe vampires are impossible fairy tales, Mr. Stoker. Literary inventions. And you are going to help us accomplish that."

Before I departed to my chambers, he showed me more of the estate. What appears to be a gentleman's library contains maps marking locations worldwide, crystalline formations housed in cases of glass, weapons that gleam with something beyond mere polish. Through one doorway I glimpsed young men training in combat forms I had never witnessed, not even in the most exotic theatrical productions.

"Weston Hall is more than my ancestral home," he whispered. "It is a fortress. A headquarters. A last line of defense against threats most of humanity will never know exist. My family has held this duty since the Conquest. God willing, we shall hold it for centuries more."

I have not yet given my answer. He does not press for one. "Consider carefully," he said as I retired. "What I ask is not small. But neither is what hangs in the balance."

The weight of this secret sits heavy on my chest tonight. I cannot sleep. The thing in the jar haunts my thoughts. Can such creatures truly exist? Yet I saw it with my own eyes.

And if they exist, what else lurks in the shadows of our world?

***

24th June, 1888

Weston Hall - The Deep Archives

This morning, His Grace led me deeper into Weston Hall than I ventured yesterday. We descended past the vault where the specimen is kept, down stone stairs worn smooth by centuries of footsteps, until we reached a level that must predate even the Norman construction.

"The Saxons had a watchtower here," as he explained, his lamp casting dancing shadows on ancient walls. "And before them, perhaps, the Romans. Perhaps even older still. This land has been guarded for longer than England has existed as a nation."

We entered a circular chamber carved from living rock. Maps covered every surface—some drawn on vellum, some on parchment, some carved directly into the stone walls themselves. In the center stood a table of black stone, inlaid with the symbol of twin moons in what appeared to be silver.

"I want you to understand," the Duke said, setting his lamp carefully, "that what we're asking of you is not new. The Weston family has been fighting this war for nearly a millennium. Your novel is simply the latest stratagem in a conflict older than your language."

He moved to a map carved into the western wall—faded lines showing routes across the North Sea. "It began with my ancestor, Rollo. You know him as the Viking chieftain who founded Normandy."

"In 911," I said, recalling my history.

"The official history tells of a peace treaty with Charles the Simple. Rollo receives land in exchange for ceasing his raids." His hand traced the carved routes with one scarred finger. "The truth is more complex. Rollo wasn't raiding for plunder by then—he was fleeing."

He moved to another map, this one showing Scandinavia. "In the frozen North, during one of his expeditions into the interior, Rollo's men disturbed something that had lain dormant for centuries. These creatures—we call them Namtar—preserved in ice since some ancient catastrophe. When the ice broke, they awoke. And they were hungry."

I felt cold despite the closeness of the chamber. "They followed him south."

"They followed the blood. Rollo's crew carried genetic markers—descendants of ancient survivors who'd settled in the North. The Namtar tracked them like hounds tracking a scent. When Rollo reached Normandy, he brought more than warriors. He brought a plague of night feeders."

The Duke pulled out a scroll, carefully unrolling it on the stone table. The document was written in a mixture of Old Norse and Latin, accompanied by crude but disturbing illustrations.

"Rollo's own account," he said. "Kept by the family. Never translated, never shared. He describes creatures that hunted his ships at night. Men who disappeared during shore leave. Warriors who returned... changed. Drinking blood. Growing stronger. No longer themselves."

I leaned closer, studying the illustrations. They showed humanoid figures with elongated limbs, black eyes, mouths opened to reveal rows of teeth. In the margins, Norse runes spelled out warnings.

Nattfjárs. Skuggaverur. Blóðþyrstur.

"Night demons. Shadow beings. Blood-thirsters," the Duke translated. "Every culture has names for them. Because they've plagued humanity since Atlantis fell."

He moved to another section of the chamber, where a genealogical chart covered an entire wall—hand-drawn over centuries, names branching like a great tree.

"The Frankish king's advisors were part of an ancient organization—the Arete," he continued. "Guardians who have fought these creatures since before recorded history. They recognized what Rollo faced. They made him an offer: land in Normandy in exchange for containing the threat. His conversion to Christianity was a cover for his initiation into the Arete."

"He became a guardian," I said.

"He became a commander. His task: establish a defensive position in Normandy, hunt down the Namtar that had followed him, and prevent them from spreading further south into Francia. Over thirty years, he succeeded. But not without cost. He lost two sons to the creatures. Dozens of his best warriors."

The Duke moved to a genealogical chart covering an entire wall—hand-drawn over centuries, names branching like a great tree.

"And he learned something crucial," he continued, pointing to specific names. "To fight the Namtar effectively, you need more than courage and silver weapons. You need the right bloodline. Certain individuals—those descended from specific ancient lineages—have natural resistance to Namtar influence. They cannot be easily turned. And more importantly, these individuals can sense the Namtar before others can."

"Bloodline sensitives," I said, the term feeling strange to my tongue.

"Exactly. Rollo spent years searching for such individuals. And eventually, the Arete found one—a young woman descended from an ancient line that traced back to the first refugees from a civilization we call Atlantis, though that name is likely corrupted through time."

His finger moved down the chart to a name written in different script: *Herleva of Falaise*.

"My direct ancestor. History calls her a tanner's daughter—the mother of William the Bastard. In truth, she was the culmination of a breeding program that had taken generations. Her lineage carried markers from the most ancient bloodlines. She was, genetically speaking, as close to a pure bloodline sensitive as had been produced in centuries."

He pulled out another scroll—a genealogy written in elegant script, showing Herleva's lineage stretching back through shadowy names to a single point: *Alyosha, First Guardian*.

"Robert, Duke of Normandy, was Arete. When his advisors discovered Herleva, they arranged for the meeting. What history records as scandalous liaison was actually carefully planned union. Robert knew exactly what she was. What their child could be."

"William," I breathed.

"William the Bastard. Mocked for his illegitimate birth, forced to fight for every scrap of respect." The Duke's voice carried an edge of anger. "But there was nothing illegitimate about him. He was deliberately created to be precisely what we needed—a warrior with the strength and tactical brilliance of the Norman dukes, combined with the supernatural sensitivity of the ancient bloodlines."

He showed me a private letter from Robert to his Arete superiors, dated 1028:

"The child exhibits signs earlier than anticipated. His nurse reports that he cries when carried near the old barrow on the north side—the one we suspect contains dormant specimens. The bloodline runs true. He will be formidable."

"William could sense them from childhood," he said. "His foster father—also Arete—trained the boy in combat techniques specifically designed for hunting these creatures. By fifteen, William had killed his first Namtar. By twenty, he'd led raids on three nests."

He moved to a map of England, circa 1066.

"Which brings us to the Conquest. History tells it as succession dispute—Harold claims the throne, William disputes it, battle ensues. But the real situation was far more desperate."

The Duke traced locations on the map, each marked with a small symbol.

"Edward the Confessor was Arete. During his reign, he maintained defensive networks established by the Saxons. But by 1065, he was dying with no heir. The Saxon Arete were in disarray—traditionalists refusing to adapt. And the Namtar were probing England's defenses, finding them weak."

He pointed to multiple marked locations. "Small outbreaks, quickly contained, but the pattern was clear. When Edward died in January 1066, the supernatural defenses collapsed. Harold Godwinson became king, but he was not Arete. Worse, he actively rejected Norman offers of assistance."

"So William invaded," I said.

"William's invasion wasn't about a crown, Mr. Stoker. It was a rescue mission. The Norman army that landed at Pevensey Bay was composed largely of Arete operatives and bloodline warriors. The Battle of Hastings was fought on two fronts—the conventional battle you read in histories, and simultaneously, another conflict beneath the visible war. When Harold fell—that famous death by arrow in the eye?"

"It wasn't an arrow," I said slowly.

"It was a Namtar that had infiltrated the Saxon lines. One of Arete, fighting under William's banner, killed both the creature and the corrupted Harold simultaneously. The arrow story explained the inexplicable."

He rolled up the documents and moved to one final piece. He pulled out a scroll—a genealogy that made my head spin. Names stretching back through Rollo to chieftains I'd never heard of. And running parallel, another line: Lapitan names, he called them. Ancient bloodlines from before recorded history..

His finger traced down through the names to William's children. "William's eldest son, Robert Curthose, became Duke of Normandy. His younger brother Henry became King of England. But Robert had two sons—Richard and William, both born outside marriage. The official histories barely mention them. A few lines in the chronicles, then silence."

He tapped the genealogy. "That silence was deliberate. These boys were brought to England in 1066, while still young. Raised here, at Weston Hall, which William established specifically for this purpose. They were the first bloodline sensitives to be trained from childhood in the family seat. The first to grow up knowing what they were, what they would become."

"Why keep them secret?" I asked.

"Because they were weapons, Mr. Stoker. Bred specifically to fight the Namtar. If that became known—if rivals understood what they truly were—they would have been targets. So they hid them in plain sight. Illegitimate sons, tucked away in Sussex, forgotten by history."

He pulled out another document—a deed, written in Norman French, dated 1066. "William granted this land for the establishment of what appeared to be a minor estate. In reality, it was a training ground, a fortress, a headquarters. Richard and William lived here their entire lives, venturing out only to hunt Namtar across Britain and the continent. They died fighting—Richard in 1079, William in 1087—but not before training the next generation."

His finger traced down through centuries of names, through Crusades and plagues, through wars I recognized and some I didn't. "From those two boys to me, unbroken. Every main-line generation born at Weston Hall. Every child raised knowing the truth. Every warrior trained in these halls before venturing out to fight. The bloodline holds. And it continues through my son, and his sons after him."

"But I'm not a warrior," I breathed.

"No," the Duke agreed. "You're something rarer—a strategist who fights with words instead of steel. Rollo had his axe. William had his sword. You have your pen. Each weapon appropriate to its age."

Above the archway leading from the chamber, I noticed the family crest carved into the stone—a shield bearing twin moons, crowned with a lion rampant, elaborate foliate scrollwork surrounding it. Beneath, a banner proclaimed: *In Umbra Lucis.*

"Our family motto. In shadow, light. We operate in shadow so that others may live in light. We bear terrible knowledge so that the innocent may remain ignorant. And, we fight monsters so that children may sleep peacefully in their beds."

He began leading me back toward the surface. "I don't require your answer today, Mr. Stoker. Consider what you've learned. Consider what hangs in the balance. When you're ready—whether that's a week or a year—let me know."

***

25th June, 1888

London

I have returned to the Lyceum, to Florence, to the comfortable rhythms of theatrical management. Irving is in good form; the current production is running smoothly. To all appearances, my life continues as before.

Yet everything has changed.

I find myself unable to concentrate on ledgers and rehearsal schedules. My mind returns constantly to the vault at Weston Hall, to the preserved creature in its jar, to the Duke's steady voice explaining impossibilities as ordinary facts. And deeper still—to that chamber from living rock, to maps spanning centuries, to the terrible truth that humanity has been protected by secret guardians for longer than our histories record.

William the Conqueror, one of history's most famous kings, was bred specifically to fight monsters. His entire life—the struggles, the victories, the conquest of England—all of it secretly in service of a war against creatures that should not exist.

How many other great figures were Arete? How much of what we call history is actually the visible surface of this hidden war?

Florence asked this evening if I was well. I assured her I was merely tired from the journey. Another lie. I am becoming familiar with those.

The commission weighs upon me. He wants me to write a novel—not any novel, but a specific lie designed to bury truth. And I find myself already composing scenes in my mind. A Transylvanian count. An English solicitor. A tale that would make the world forget real monsters.

In Umbra Lucis. In shadow, light.

Perhaps there are different kinds of courage. Perhaps the pen can be as mighty as the sword, though in ways I never imagined.

I have not yet decided. But I know, in my bones, that I will eventually say yes.

***

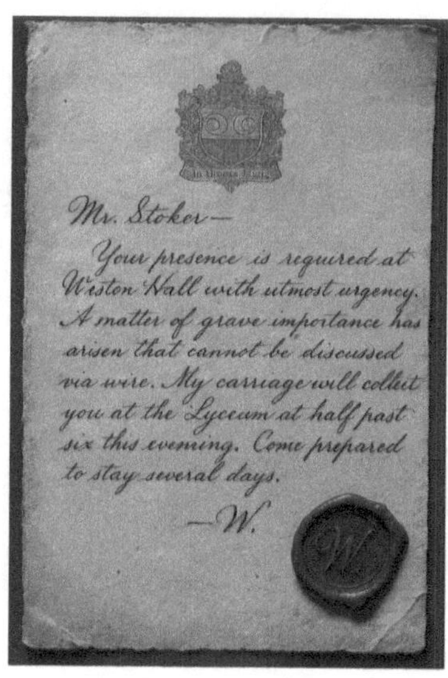

Mr. Stoker—

Your presence is required at Wiston Hall with utmost urgency. A matter of grave importance has arisen that cannot be discussed via wire. My carriage will collect you at the Lyceum at half past six this evening. Come prepared to stay several days.

—W.

***

16th September, 1888

London, Evening

The second Whitechapel murder has the city in a state of panic I haven't witnessed since the Fenian bombings. Women won't venture out after dark. The police are overwhelmed. The newspapers compete to print the most lurid details.

I've read every account I could find. Not from morbid fascination, though Florence clearly thinks that's the reason for my intense interest.

I'm studying them because of what the Duke taught me at Weston Hall.

"You'll need to learn the difference, Mr. Stoker," he'd said, showing me photographs of genuine Namtar attacks disguised as other causes. "Between what we fight and what humanity does to itself. The patterns are distinct once you know what to look for."

The Whitechapel murders are public. Theatrical. The bodies left on display for maximum shock. The mutilations serve no purpose beyond horror.

The Namtar, from everything I've learned, are the opposite. Efficient. Clean. Their victims simply disappear, or die of "mysterious illness," or suffer "tragic accidents." No spectacle. No terror. Just quiet, methodical feeding.

Still, I needed confirmation. I sent a carefully worded telegram to Sussex this morning.

His reply was characteristically brief: "Confirmed human. Arete not involved. Continue your studies."

Your studies. As if what I'm doing is academic. As if I haven't spent three months trying to process what I witnessed in that vault.

But I'm grateful for the confirmation. The shadows I see everywhere now—at least these particular shadows are ordinary human evil.

Somehow, that's almost worse.

1889

July, 1889

London

A newspaper article caught my eye today whilst taking breakfast. A brief mention, buried on page seven, about "unexplained circumstances" surrounding deaths in Yorkshire several years past. The article referenced the "Whitby incidents of 1885" and wondered whether recent strange occurrences near the coast might be related.

I read it three times, my coffee growing cold.

The Duke was right. The stories persist. They evolve. They spread like creeping vine, and no amount of official denials can kill them. People whisper. They remember. They connect patterns that should remain unconnected.

I clipped the article and placed it in my desk drawer. Evidence. Or perhaps ammunition for the work ahead.

I have begun reading everything I can find on folklore—vampires, night creatures, legends of the undead. Not for the Lyceum, though that's what I tell anyone who asks. But to understand what people already believe, so I might craft something more compelling.

The research fascinates me, even as I know I'm being drawn deeper into this dark web.

***

8th September, 1889

London

Nearly three months since my visit to Weston Hall. The Duke has not pressed for an answer, which somehow makes the decision heavier. He knows I will come to it in my own time.

I wrote to him today with questions—about the organization he called the Arete, about how widespread these Namtar truly are, about what would happen if humanity learned the truth. His reply came within four days:

"Mr. Stoker - Your questions demonstrate the thoughtfulness I hoped for. Visit again when your schedule permits. There is much more to show you. - Weston"

Brief, but the invitation clear. He's patient. This is a war measured in centuries, after all. What are a few months?

Irving has me occupied with preparations for the autumn season. But I find my thoughts wandering during rehearsals. What if he's right? What if a well-crafted fiction could protect millions?

Is it not the role of the writer to illuminate truth? Yet here I'm being asked to obscure it.

The moral question torments me.

***

3rd October, 1889

Weston Hall

I returned to Sussex today, unable to resist the pull of unanswered questions. His Grace welcomed me as though my arrival was expected—perhaps it was. He strikes me as a man who anticipates much.

This visit, he showed me the archives proper—not the deep chambers of before, but rooms filled with documents, reports, photographs, illustrations. Evidence spanning decades of a war fought in secret.

Maps showing incidents across Britain and Europe. And photographs—blurred but unmistakable—of recent combat sites, of creatures, of warriors who gave their lives.

One photograph particularly struck me: a gravestone in Whitby, St. Mary's churchyard. "William Thorne - Died in Service, 28 July 1885." The official record claims he died in a fall. The Duke told me the truth—his throat torn open, buying time for others to kill the creature.

He was twenty-eight years old.

"Every generation pays the price," he said quietly. "My father four years ago. Thorne and others before him. Countless warriors whose names are recorded here but nowhere else. They died so that others might live in ignorance—blissful, safe ignorance."

He showed me something else—a journal kept by Miss Adelaide Marsh, an archivist. Page after page documenting incidents worldwide, the Arete responses, the containment efforts, the careful construction of cover stories.

I asked the Duke what would happen if people knew the truth.

"Panic," he said simply. "Witch hunts. They would start killing anyone who seemed different. The very people we protect—those with bloodline sensitivity—would be first targets. And in that chaos, the real threats would flourish unseen."

"So you lie to protect them."

"We lie to protect everyone, Mr. Stoker. Including those who would hunt us if they knew what we were."

I departed Weston Hall with my head full of terrible knowledge. The weight grows heavier, not lighter.

***

20th December, 1889

London

So many months since that first summons. Carrying this secret, turning it over in my mind like a puzzle that refuses to resolve.

The year draws to a close. Christmas approaches. Florence and I will spend it with family, surrounded by warmth and laughter and blessed ignorance of what lurks beyond the firelight.

I have not yet given my answer. But I know it will be yes. How can it not be? I have seen the evidence. I have held in my hands the proof that humanity is protected by shadows I never knew existed.

If my pen can serve that protection—if I can craft a lie beautiful enough to bury the truth—how can I refuse?

The question is not whether I will do it. The question is when I will admit to myself that the decision is already made.

I understand those words now. They are not merely a motto. They are a burden, willingly carried.

And I am about to shoulder my portion of it.

1890

1

4th February, 1890

London

I have done it.

This morning, I wrote to His Grace and accepted his commission. The words came easier than expected, perhaps because they merely formalized what my heart had already decided months ago.

"Your Grace - I have given your proposal the consideration it deserves. The weight of what you ask is not lost on me, nor is the necessity of it. I accept. Tell me what you need me to do, and I shall do it to the best of my abilities. Yours in service, Abraham Stoker."

The letter went by afternoon post. There is finality in it—like signing a contract with forces I don't fully comprehend. But also relief. The decision is made. No more wrestling with it in the small hours.

Florence asked why I seemed lighter today. I told her I'd finally committed to the new book project I'd been considering. Not entirely a lie—simply an incomplete truth.

I am becoming adept at those.

Now I wait for a response and whatever instructions follow. I have placed myself in service to a cause I barely understand, to fight an enemy most people think is myth.

God help me, I hope I'm capable of what they need.

***

2nd March, 1890

London

His Grace's reply arrived this morning, delivered again by that same liveried messenger:

"Mr. Stoker - Your decision honors us. The work begins in earnest now. I propose a research expedition to Whitby in the coming summer—the site where this current crisis originated. It will provide atmosphere for your novel while allowing you to understand fully what occurred there. Dr. Clarence Hartwell will meet you and provide guidance. I shall arrange all details. Await further correspondence. - Weston"

So it begins. A "research trip" to Whitby, where twelve people died in 1885. Where the newspapers asked questions that still echo.

I will walk those streets. Climb those steps. Stand where horror unfolded.

And from it, I will craft a beautiful lie.

***

18th April, 1890

London

The arrangements are made. I depart for Whitby on the 26th of July—three months hence. The Duke has been thorough in his preparations. A packet arrived yesterday containing:

Railway tickets (first class, which Florence noted with approval) Reservation at a respectable hotel overlooking the harbor A slim volume titled "Maritime Legends of the Yorkshire Coast" Calling card for Dr. Clarence Hartwell Brief note: "Familiarize yourself with the volume. Dr. H. has much to show you. -W"

I opened the book expecting typical folklore collection—sailors' superstitions, ghost stories, the usual fare. But reading more carefully, certain passages struck me as oddly specific. Descriptions of creatures. Behaviors. Patterns of attack. And marginal notes in his precise hand, directing my attention: "Note the timing" beside nocturnal disappearances. "Observe the progression" next to accounts of mysterious illness spreading through households.

This is not folklore. This is field research, disguised as folklore.

Irving has granted me a fortnight away during the summer lull. I told him it was for atmospheric research for a Gothic novel I'm planning. He approved enthusiastically—thinks it will be good for me to escape London's heat.

Florence is pleased I'm taking proper holiday. She wants to visit her family in Dublin while I'm north. I encouraged this. Better she's away, enjoying herself, than watching me lie badly about what I'm truly doing in Whitby.

Three months to prepare. Three months to steel myself for walking streets where people died horribly. For learning truths I cannot unlearn.

***

25th May, 1890

London

Two months until Whitby. I find myself increasingly distracted at the Lyceum. Irving noticed yesterday that I'd approved an expense twice—something I never do. He asked if I was feeling well.

"Simply preoccupied with the new project," I told him. True enough, though he has no idea what that project truly is.

I have been reading the Maritime Legends volume repeatedly, studying those marginal notes. The Duke has essentially given me a coded field guide to Namtar behavior, hidden within seemingly innocent folklore. Anyone else would read it as interesting local legends. I read it as a catalog of hunting patterns, feeding cycles, transformation symptoms.

There's a particular account of deaths in a coastal village in 1847—forty-three years ago. The official explanation cited contaminated fish. But the note reads: "Three scouts. Contained after seventeen deaths, including my father's. Too many witnesses. Story required careful construction."

Seventeen people died. And history records it as bad fish.

How many other "natural disasters" and "unfortunate coincidences" are actually Namtar incidents? How much of what we accept as mundane tragedy is actually supernatural horror, carefully disguised?

Florence asked what I was reading so intently. I showed her the cover. "Research for the novel—Yorkshire legends." She smiled and kissed my cheek, pleased I was taking the work seriously.

If she knew the truth...

But that's precisely the point, isn't it? She must never know. None of them must.

***

22nd July, 1890

On the train to Whitby

The Yorkshire landscape rolls past my window—green hills giving way to moorland, wild and windswept. The further north we travel, the more I feel I am journeying not through space but through time, away from gaslit London toward something older and stranger.

I have the compartment to myself, thankfully. The Maritime Legends volume lies open on my lap, though I have read it so many times I could recite passages. Each reading reveals more. What seemed like ordinary folklore on first pass now reads like carefully disguised truth.

The account of "the Whitby Terror" from July 1885 takes up three pages. Officially: twelve deaths over three weeks, attributed to "unfortunate accidents and coincidental illness." But the marginalia tells another story:

"Scout. Solo operative. Tracked victims by bloodline markers." "Arete response deployed 22 July. Containment achieved 28 July." "Specimen preserved. See Archives, Vault 3."

That specimen is what I saw at Weston Hall. One of twelve victims' killer, now reduced to an object of study in a jar of spirits.

The train passes through a cutting, and for a moment the light fails, plunging the compartment into shadow. When we emerge again into afternoon sun, I realize my hands are trembling.

I am going to the site of a massacre. To walk the streets they walked. To climb steps they climbed. To stand where their killer stood.

And from this, I am to craft romantic entertainment.

The moral weight of it sits heavy in my chest. But I have committed.

***

27th July, 1890

Whitby, Evening

I have arrived as the sun set over the harbor, painting the ruined abbey on the eastern cliff in shades of blood and gold. The town is smaller than I expected, more intimate. Every street, every building feels knowable, which somehow makes the knowledge I carry more terrible.

Twelve people died here. In this small town where everyone knows everyone. Where the fishwives recognize which boats are whose, where shopkeepers know their regular customers, where children play in narrow lanes.

And something hunted them.

My lodgings overlook the harbor—a respectable hotel, as the Duke promised. The landlady, Mrs. Patterson, was kind in that particular way of Yorkshire people, speaking little but ensuring I had everything

needed. When I mentioned I was a writer researching local atmosphere, she nodded approvingly.

"We've a rich history here, sir. The abbey, the old stories. Though..."
she paused, straightening the curtains. "Some stories are best left in the
past, if you take my meaning."

"The incidents of 1885?" I ventured.

Her face closed. "Sad business, that. Best forgotten. Though some
folk still whisper about that summer. I'd steer clear of it, were I you.
Nothing there but grief."

After she left, I stood at the window. The abbey ruins loom against
the darkening sky, stark and somehow watchful. Tomorrow, Dr.
Hartwell will call at ten o'clock. Tomorrow, my education in the true
horror of Whitby begins.

Tonight, I cannot sleep. The sea air smells of salt and fish and something indefinable—perhaps simply the weight of history, of stories
layered upon stories, of truths buried beneath accepted explanations.

***

28th July, 1890

Whitby

Dr. Clarence Hartwell arrived precisely at ten o'clock—a man of
perhaps fifty years, lean and weathered, with the careful movements
of someone accustomed to handling dangerous things. He carried
a walking stick and a leather satchel, and his eyes assessed me with
clinical interest.

"Mr. Stoker," he said without preamble. "I understand His Grace has shown you a specimen. Good. That will make today's work easier. Shall we walk?"

We walked.

He led me through Whitby's streets as if conducting a lecture on architecture rather than describing a series of murders. His voice remained steady, almost bored, as he recounted horror.

"The first victim was discovered here, behind the fish market. Mary Thornton, aged forty-three, mother of two. Found at dawn by her husband. Two small punctures at the throat—easily attributed to sharp implement or animal bite. The local physician was puzzled but certified death by misadventure."

We walked on.

"The second, third, and fourth deaths occurred within the same week. Different locations, but a pattern emerged for those trained to see it. All showed signs of gradual deterioration before death. Pallor. Weakness. Strange somnambulism at night. The families reported seeing their loved ones changed—colder, somehow. Less themselves."

He paused at a narrow alley. "The fifth victim was found here. A child, Mr. Stoker. Seven years old. That was when His Grace's father realized this was not random predation but something targeted and intelligent."

My throat had gone dry. "How did you know? How did the Arete know it was... what it was?"

The doctor smiled thinly. "Because we've been fighting them for a thousand years. We know the signs. And more importantly, we have equipment to detect them."

He withdrew a peculiar device from his satchel—brass and glass, with intricate mechanisms I could not fathom. It resembled a compass, but instead of magnetic north, its needle pointed toward... something else.

"A resonance detector," he explained. "Primitive compared to what we'll develop, but adequate for field work. It reads crystalline energy signatures—specifically, the corrupted frequencies that Namtar emit."

He held the device at arm's length and walked slowly down the alley. The needle swung wildly, then settled, pointing toward the harbor.

"Even after five years, the resonance lingers. These creatures leave impressions. Like footprints in wet sand, but in the fabric of energy itself." He returned the device to his satchel. "That is how we tracked it. It fed here, moved there, rested elsewhere. We mapped its hunting pattern over three weeks."

"Why not stop it sooner?"

His expression darkened. "Because we did not realize what we faced until the fifth death. By then, we were racing to understand its pattern before it completed its feeding cycle. And Mr. Stoker, you must understand—these things are intelligent. Cunning. It knew it was being hunted and adapted accordingly."

We climbed the one hundred and ninety-nine steps to St. Mary's Church and the abbey ruins. I counted each one, my breath coming harder as we ascended. Dr. Hartwell climbed with steady, practiced ease.

"The creature roosted here during daylight hours," he said when we reached the summit. Wind whipped at our coats, carrying cries of gulls. "A popular misconception—that they fear the sun. They don't fear it, but they are weakened by it. Nocturnal by nature—they hunt at night, rest during day. They were created to live in the darkness—that's when their prey is vulnerable and they're at their strongest."

He led me to a particular section of the ruins, behind a crumbling wall. The ancient stone showed marks I initially took for weathering.

"Look closer."

I knelt. The marks were gouges—deep scratches scored into stone that had stood for centuries. The pattern too regular to be natural erosion, too purposeful to be accidental.

"It was resting here when we cornered it," Dr. Hartwell said quietly. "The twenty-eighth of July, 1885. Five years ago today, in fact. Four of us: myself, James Caldwell, William Thorne, and His Grace, Edmund Weston."

He touched the gouges in the stone. "This is where Thorne died. The creature was weakened but still formidable. It moved faster than any living thing I have witnessed. Caldwell managed to sever one of its arms with a silver blade—that slowed it enough for His Grace to land the killing blow. Beheading. It's the only way to be certain."

"And the body?" My voice sounded strange in my own ears.

"Preserved. You've seen it."

The wind carried the scent of the sea, and for a moment I could almost imagine it—four men in this place at dawn, facing something that should not exist. The fear. The violence. The death.

"Why are you showing me this?" I asked.

He turned to face me fully. "Because His Grace wants you to understand the stakes. You're not simply writing a story. You're creating a shield. Every detail you include that's false, every weakness you invent, every rule you establish—it all serves to obscure the truth. When the next horror is unleashed, people will eventually compare it to your creation and declare it impossible. Your Count Dracula, with his aristocratic airs and his fear of garlic, will make the real thing unbelievable."

He gestured to the town below. "Those twelve victims? Their deaths were eventually attributed to mysterious illness. The newspapers speculated about contaminated water, perhaps rare disease.

People accepted these explanations because the truth was too terrible. But the questions lingered. The rumors spread. Your job is to ensure that when people hear 'vampire,' they think of your fiction—not of Mary Thornton found behind the fish market, or of a seven-year-old child drained of life, or of desperate men fighting a monster atop these cliffs."

He showed me the newspaper coverage from five years ago. I have kept the clipping. "Tragic fall," I said, reading the account of Thorne's death. "That was the official story," Dr. Hartwell replied. "The truth is in the Arete archives."

He showed me the preserved article with clinical detachment, but as we prepared to leave, he paused at the door.

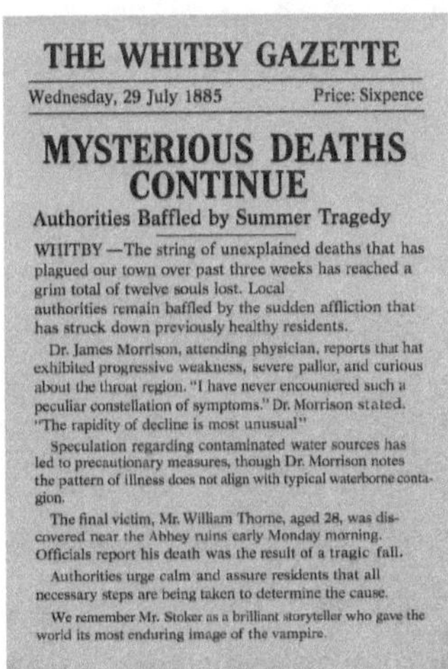

THE WHITBY GAZETTE

Wednesday, 29 July 1885 — Price: Sixpence

MYSTERIOUS DEATHS CONTINUE

Authorities Baffled by Summer Tragedy

WHITBY —The string of unexplained deaths that has plagued our town over past three weeks has reached a grim total of twelve souls lost. Local authorities remain baffled by the sudden affliction that has struck down previously healthy residents.

Dr. James Morrison, attending physician, reports that hat exhibited progressive weakness, severe pallor, and curious about the throat region. "I have never encountered such a peculiar constellation of symptoms." Dr. Morrison stated. "The rapidity of decline is most unusual"

Speculation regarding contaminated water sources has led to precautionary measures, though Dr. Morrison notes the pattern of illness does not align with typical waterborne contagion.

The final victim, Mr. William Thorne, aged 28, was discovered near the Abbey ruins early Monday morning. Officials report his death was the result of a tragic fall.

Authorities urge calm and assure residents that all necessary steps are being taken to determine the cause.

We remember Mr. Stoker as a brilliant storyteller who gave the world its most enduring image of the vampire.

Whitby Gazette

"I have a daughter," he said quietly. "She's eight. Asks why Papa is always away. I tell her it's scientific research." He looked back at the vault. "Not entirely untrue. But she'll never know what I protect her from."

I understood, then, that we all carry this burden differently. Some with pen. Some with scalpel. All with silence.

But, why did His Grace not tell me he was there? That he fought personally in this battle? He showed me the preserved specimen, told me about the twelve deaths, but never mentioned that he himself wielded the blade that killed it.

Perhaps that is simply the way of commanders—they speak of the mission, not their own role in it. Or perhaps the memory is too painful. He lost a good man that day. William Thorne, twenty-eight years old, gave his life so Weston could deliver the killing blow.

In Umbra Lucis. The Duke lives that motto—standing in shadow, his own heroism hidden even from those he recruits to the cause.

***

28th July, 1890

Whitby, Evening

Dr. Hartwell departed after our tour, leaving me with a leather folio containing documents I am to study. I have spread them across my writing desk, and the contents are both fascinating and horrifying.

Medical reports from the attending physician, noting symptoms he could not explain. Avoiding supernatural claims but describing "strange figures" and "unnatural occurrences." A map of Whitby with each victim's location marked, showing a clear pattern radiating from the harbor toward the abbey.

Sketches of the creature, drawn from examination of the preserved specimen—anatomical studies showing bone structure, dental arrangement, the way joints articulate beyond human capacity.

And photographs. Actual photographs, though somewhat blurred, of the combat site atop the cliffs. I can make out figures—men with weapons—and something else, a shape that seems to resist the camera's ability to capture it clearly, as if it exists partially outside normal perception.

One photograph, the one I saw at Weston Hall: William Thorne's grave marker.

I am meant to transform this—all this horror, sacrifice, desperate violence—into a romantic tale that will hide the truth.

Can I do it? Should I do it?

A knock at my door interrupted these thoughts. The landlady's boy, delivering a telegram:

WELL DONE STOP DR H REPORTS SATISFACTORY PROGRESS STOP CONTINUE OBSERVATIONS THREE MORE DAYS STOP RETURN WESTON HALL 3 AUGUST STOP REAL WORK BEGINS STOP W

Three more days in Whitby. Three days to walk these streets, to absorb atmosphere, to understand the setting where people died and where my fictional vampire must now arrive.

I looked again at the photograph of Thorne's grave. He was twenty-eight years old when he died fighting a monster. I am forty-three, a theatre manager who has never done anything braver than face an angry dramatist.

Yet I am being asked to fight the same enemy—not with silver blades or golden light, but with words.

The battlefield may be smaller, but the war remains the same.

***

29th July, 1890

Whitby

I spent today walking the town alone, following the route Dr. Hartwell traced yesterday but at my own pace, absorbing details. Whitby is a remarkable place—the harbor with its fishing boats, the narrow streets climbing the hillside, the looming presence of the abbey ruins against the sky. There is natural drama to the setting, a Gothic atmosphere that requires no embellishment.

I climbed the one hundred and ninety-nine steps again, slower this time, imagining a young woman making this climb at night, drawn by something she doesn't understand. Lucy Westenra, I think I shall call her. A sweet girl, innocent, destroyed by the very monster that should have—but that's the fiction I must create. Monsters with rules. Predictable. Knowable. Defeatable.

At the summit, I sat on a bench near St. Mary's Church and made notes:

The approach by sea—dramatic arrival
The creature coming ashore in the form of a great hound
The abbey ruins as his first resting place in England
Lucy as his initial victim—proximity, opportunity
The town's response—confusion, medical explanations

I am already transforming reality into fiction. The Namtar that came to Whitby arrived on a fishing vessel, stowed away, drawn by instinct for bloodlines. But in my story, it shall arrive on a ship called

Demeter, a ghost ship crashed upon shore with dead crew and a black dog running from its deck.

More dramatic. More Gothic. More obviously impossible.

I met an old sailor at the harbor this afternoon, quite by accident. He was mending nets and proved talkative when I showed interest. I asked, casually, if he remembered anything unusual from summer five years past.

His face darkened. "Strange summer, that was. Deaths, you know. People said it was bad water, but I knew some of them that died. Healthy folk one day, wasting away the next. And the lights."

"Lights?"

"Aye, lights up at the abbey ruins. Dancing lights, like nothing I'd seen. And my nets that summer—kept finding them torn to pieces, like something powerful had thrashed through them." He shook his head. "But they said it was contaminated water. Easier to believe, I suppose."

"Do you believe it was contaminated water?"

He looked at me shrewdly. "I believe in what I can see and touch, sir. But I also know there's things in this world that don't fit into neat explanations. My gran used to tell stories about night walkers—old country superstitions, brought over from elsewhere way back. But sometimes old superstitions exist for a reason."

I thanked him and walked back to my lodgings with a notebook full of details: the way light falls on the water, the sound of gulls, the salt smell mixing with fish and tar, the steep streets, the weathered faces of people who make their living from the sea.

All of it shall go into my book. But twisted. Transformed. Made safely fictional.

***

31st July, 1890

Whitby

My final full day here. I visited the public library this morning, a handsome building near the harbor. The librarian showed me their collection of local histories and folklore volumes.

Among them, I found exactly what I'd hoped for: William Wilkinson's *Account of the Principalities of Wallachia and Moldavia*. I opened it at random and found a footnote that sent a chill down my spine:

"DRACULA in the Wallachian language means DEVIL. The W allachians... at this day, consider the word as synonymous with terror."

Dracula. The Devil. Terror made into a name.

I copied the footnote carefully into my notebook. This is perfect—better than "Count Vampyr" or some obvious construction. Dracula carries weight, foreignness, an air of authenticity. It sounds real, which will make the fiction more convincing.

When I returned the volume, the librarian asked if I was researching folklore for a book. I told her I was considering a novel set in Yorkshire, incorporating local legends.

"How exciting," she said. "We don't get many authors visiting. Though of course, there was that terrible business five years ago. Some writers attempted sensational accounts, but nothing came of it. The truth was too mundane—contaminated water kills people just as dead as any monster."

"Indeed," I said, though I knew the truth was neither mundane nor about water.

She lowered her voice. "Though between you and me, my cousin Sarah knew one of the victims—Mary Thornton. She said Mary wasn't herself in those final days. Said she seemed... haunted. Walked the streets at night like she was in a dream. Came home with no memory of where she'd been. But the doctors said it was delirium from the contamination."

"How terrible for her family."

"Five years on, and people still whisper about that summer. Some say the deaths were too strange, too coordinated to be mere illness. But what else could they be?" She straightened the returned volumes. "We tell ourselves stories to make sense of things. Sometimes the stories we tell ourselves are kinder than the truth."

I thought of those words: *Create a vampire so compelling that it replaces the real thing in public imagination.*

"Yes," I said. "Sometimes stories are all that stand between us and things too terrible to accept."

She gave me a curious look but said nothing more.

Tonight, I packed my valise for tomorrow's departure. The folio of documents from the doctor goes with me, along with notebooks filled with observations, sketches of locations, and that copied footnote: *Dracula means devil.*

I have what I need from Whitby. Now the real work begins.

***

1st August, 1890
On the train, returning south

I departed Whitby this morning with the dawn, watching the abbey ruins recede into mist as the train carried me away. I felt unexpected sadness leaving—as if I were abandoning something important, or perhaps abandoning the twelve people who died there to being forgotten.

But that's precisely what I've been commissioned to ensure, isn't it? That they remain forgotten. That their deaths become a footnote, a minor mystery lost to time, overshadowed by a fictional Count who never existed.

The countryside passes my window again, green and peaceful under August sun. Two days until I'm expected at Weston Hall. Two days to review my notes, to organize thoughts, to prepare for whatever briefing has been arranged.

I opened the folio Dr. Hartwell gave me and studied the anatomical drawings within. Dr. Clarence Hartwell's meticulous documentation of the Whitby specimen, preserved after its destruction in 1885. I have preserved it here.

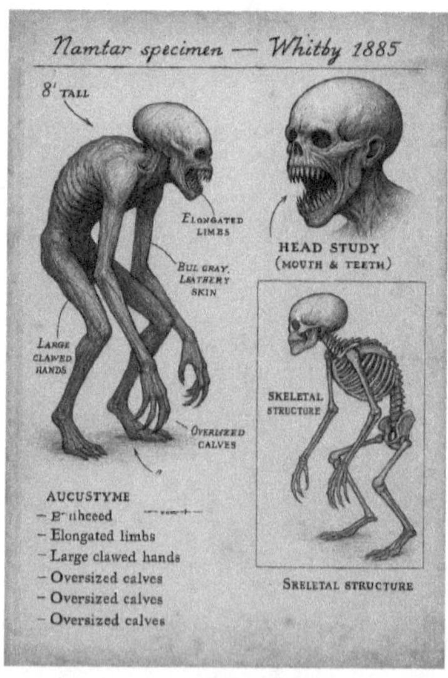

The artist rendered every detail with scientific precision. Eight feet tall in its natural crouch. The elongated limbs. The articulated joints that bend in ways human joints cannot. The bulbous skull. The dental structure showing rows of needle-like teeth designed for efficient bloodletting, not feeding.

"Dull gray leathery skin," Dr. Hartwell's notes read. "Oversized calves suggesting explosive locomotive capacity. Specimen terminated via decapitation - the only method proven effective."

This is what I must transform. This nightmare of anatomical impossibility must become Count Dracula - aristocratic, seductive, bound by rules that do not actually constrain it.

I must make this creature vulnerable to symbols and substances that cannot actually harm it. I must give readers a vampire they can defeat with garlic and crosses and sunlight, when the real horror fears none of these things.

The train passed through a tunnel, and in the sudden darkness reflected in the window, I caught my own face looking back. I looked haunted. Perhaps I am.

When we emerged again into daylight, I turned to a fresh page in my notebook and wrote:

THE STORY OF COUNT DRACULA - A Novel - By Abraham Stoker

Chapter the First: Jonathan Harker's Journal

3 May. Bistritz.—Left Munich at 8:35 P.M., on 1st May, arriving at Vienna early next morning...

I stopped after a few lines. These are false words, written to conceal truth. Yet they feel right somehow. The story wants to be told, even if every word is a lie.

Tomorrow I return to Weston Hall, where the Duke and his team will guide me in crafting this beautiful deception.

***

10th August, 1890

Weston Hall, Evening

I returned to Sussex this afternoon, welcomed by His Grace himself at the door. He looked older than when we first met—or perhaps I simply see more clearly now. The weight he carries, the centuries of duty in his family line, the knowledge of what lurks in the dark.

"Mr. Stoker," he said. "Dr. Hartwell's reports were excellent. You've seen the site, absorbed the atmosphere, understood the reality. Now we transform that reality into useful fiction."

He led me not to the vault this time, but to a different chamber—a working library set up specifically for my use. A large desk dominated the center, positioned to catch afternoon light. Shelves lined the walls, but instead of books, they held carefully organized materials:

Maps of Eastern Europe, with certain locations marked Folders containing "witness accounts" that I am to adapt Medical texts describing various blood disorders (to inspire false symptoms) Religious texts covering Christian symbols and rituals (to establish fake weaknesses) Folklore collections from multiple cultures (for atmospheric details)

And at the center of the desk, a stack of blank paper, bottles of ink, and a note in Weston's hand:

"Your workspace. Use it well. We begin tomorrow with the complete briefing. Tonight, rest. Tomorrow, we create a vampire that cannot exist."

Miss Adelaide Marsh appeared in the doorway—the archivist. She's perhaps thirty-five years, with sharp eyes and ink-stained fingers.

"Mr. Stoker," she said. "I've prepared a reading list for this evening—materials that will frame tomorrow's discussion. Nothing too heavy. Only context." She handed me a slim volume. "This one in particular. Medieval accounts of supposed vampire incidents, with my annotations showing what actually happened versus what was reported."

I thanked her and opened the book. The first annotation read:

"Reported: Victim rose from grave and attacked family.

Actual: Namtar scout mimicking the deceased's appearance to access household. Classic infiltration tactic."

Truth and lie, side by side. This is what I must learn—not only how to lie, but how to lie convincingly based on kernels of truth.

"We are historians of a war that cannot be recorded in official histories," she said. "But we remember. We must remember, so that their sacrifices matter."

The Duke returned with brandy—the same French vintage as before. "To your health, Mr. Stoker, and to the success of our endeavor. You're about to embark on the most important work of your life. Not for glory. Not for acclaim. But for the protection of millions who will never know your name or what you've done for them."

We drank.

"Tomorrow," he said, "we begin teaching you to see as we see. To understand what the Namtar truly are, so you can craft a fiction so far from truth that the two can never be confused."

My room here is comfortable—the same guest chamber as before. I can hear the wind in the ancient oaks outside. Somewhere below me, in the vault beneath this house, that preserved Namtar waits in its jar.

Tomorrow, my real education begins.

***

11th August, 1890

Weston Hall - The Working Library

The briefing began at nine o'clock sharp. His Grace, Dr. Hartwell, who arrived late last evening, and Miss Marsh assembled around the large desk, which had been cleared save for two sheets of paper positioned side by side. One was labeled **NAMTAR - CLASSIFIED TRUTH**. The other, **DRACULA - PUBLIC FICTION**.

"The Inversion Plan," the Duke announced. "Mr. Stoker, what you are about to receive is perhaps the most comprehensive knowledge of Namtar biology and behavior ever compiled. We are trusting you with centuries of hard-won intelligence. And then we are asking you to systematically lie about every single detail."

Miss Marsh dipped her pen. "I'll record as we go. This document will guide your writing—a reference sheet showing what's real and what you must invent. By day's end, you'll have a complete mythology that contradicts reality at every turn."

The doctor leaned forward. "Let's begin with the most fundamental question: What are they?"

I opened my notebook, pen ready.

"The Namtar are not supernatural," He continued. "They are biological. Engineered, in fact, though by technology we still don't fully comprehend. Created using corrupted crystal technology, they are designed as weapons—evolutionary tools meant to replace humanity."

Miss Marsh wrote under TRUTH: *Biological weapons. Engineered organisms. Purpose: Human replacement.*

Weston suggested, "Why not make them supernatural. Ancient curse, perhaps. Demonic origin. Anything that places them firmly in the realm of myth and legend rather than science."

I wrote: *Dracula = curse of the undead. Ancient evil. Folkloric, not scientific.*

We continued for hours. Their physical nature: true form seven to eight feet tall when extended, crystalline skin structure, fully black eyes when feeding. My fictional vampire: tall but human proportions, pale but distinguished, red eyes perhaps, able to blend into society.

Their feeding process: they consume life force through blood, inject crystalline pathogen that transforms victims over agonizing weeks. My version: romantic seduction, three bites for transformation, quick and tragically beautiful.

Their intelligence and organization: highly sophisticated, telepathic network, pack hunters coordinating through shared consciousness. My invention: solitary aristocrat, lone villain with no connection to others of his kind.

"This is where we truly diverge," the Duke said when we reached weaknesses. "Dr. Hartwell, what actually harms them?"

"Silver slows their healing. Beheading kills them permanently—severs the crystalline network in the spine. Fire can destroy the pathogen if applied early. Certain crystal frequencies disrupt their energy patterns, though we're perfecting that technology. That's it. Those are their only vulnerabilities."

"Not much for a novel," I observed.

"Which is why we invent more," he said. "Many more. Miss Marsh?"

She consulted her prepared list. "Based on folklore traditions: sunlight as fatal, crosses and holy water as repellent, garlic as deterrent, inability to cross running water, inability to enter dwellings without invitation, wooden stakes as lethal, mirrors not reflecting them, immunity to conventional weapons."

"But none of that is true?" I asked, though I knew the answer.

"None of it," Dr. Hartwell confirmed. "Namtar are weakened considerably by daylight—the hunters become the hunted, easily destroyed. But they're nocturnal hunters by design. They were created for darkness—that's when they're strongest. Christian symbols mean nothing to them. Garlic is irrelevant. They can cross water, enter uninvited, and are unaffected by wood. "As for mirrors—they reflect fine when physical, but cast no reflection in shadow form."

"Then why include these?"

"Because," the Duke said, "when the next incident occurs, witnesses will compare it to your fictional vampire. 'But the creature was seen in daylight,' they'll say. 'It entered the house unbidden.' And others will respond: 'Then it cannot have been a vampire. Everyone knows vampires cannot do those things.' Your fiction will make the truth unbelievable."

"They're called the Night Plague for a reason. They hunt exclusively after dark. Not from any weakness to sunlight—no burning, no withering—but because they're nocturnal predators. During daylight they rest, dormant. It's simply their nature, like owls or bats. But your Count Dracula? Make the sun *fatal* to him. Make it a weapon his enemies can use."

The elegant cruelty of it struck me. Create such specific rules that reality cannot match them.

By evening, we had our document—two columns, truth and fiction, every detail systematically inverted:

NAMTAR (TRUTH) vs **DRACULA (FICTION)**

Biological weapons →   Supernatural curse

Active at night (natural behavior) → Cannot survive sunlight (fatal weakness)

7-8 feet, inhuman proportions   → Tall but human appearance

Crystalline skin, black eyes   → Pale, red eyes

Feed on life force via blood   → Drink blood for sustenance

Agonizing transformation over   weeks → Romantic seduction

Highly intelligent pack   hunters → Solitary aristocrat

Operate in daylight → Cannot   survive sunlight

Unaffected by Christian   symbols → Repelled by crosses

No issues with garlic/water →   Deterred by garlic, cannot cross water

Created as weapons →   Demonic/folkloric origin

Miss Marsh prepared the final comparison document—two columns, truth versus fiction, laid out with frightening clarity. I have preserved a copy here, evidence of what we have done. Looking at it complete, I feel the weight of every lie.

She organized her documents with practiced efficiency. I noticed she wore a mourning ring—black enamel, discreet. "My brother," she said, catching my glance. "Dover, 1882. Namtar scout." She returned to her papers. "This is why precision matters, Mr. Stoker. Every false rule you create might save someone's brother."

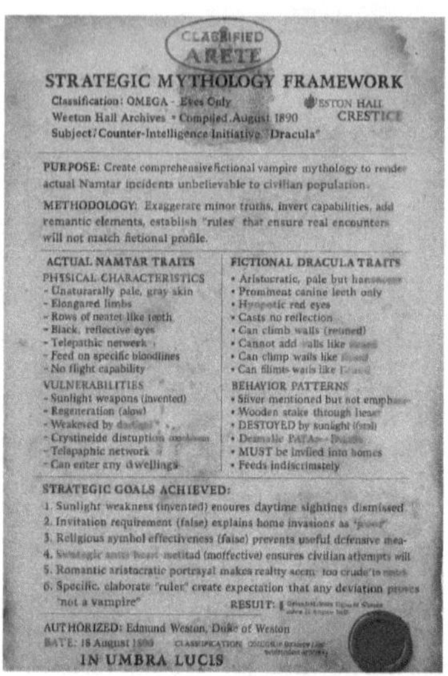

CLASSIFIED
ARETE

STRATEGIC MYTHOLOGY FRAMEWORK

Classification: OMEGA - Eyes Only   WESTON HALL
Weeton Hall Archives • Compiled August 1890   CRESTICE
Subject: Counter-Intelligence Initiative "Dracula"

PURPOSE: Create comprehensive fictional vampire mythology to render actual Namtar incidents unbelievable to civilian population.

METHODOLOGY: Exaggerate minor truths, invert capabilities, add romantic elements, establish "rules" that ensure real encounters will not match fictional profile.

ACTUAL NAMTAR TRAITS	FICTIONAL DRACULA TRAITS
PHYSICAL CHARACTERISTICS	• Aristocratic, pale but handsome
- Unaturarally pale, gray skin	• Prominent canine teeth only
- Elongared limbs	• Hypnotic red eyes
- Rows of neatet like teeth	• Casts no reflection
- Black, reflective eyes	• Can climb walls (retined)
- Telepathic network	• Cannot add walls like
- Feed on specific bloodlines	• Can climp walls like
- No flight capability	• Can filimts walls like
VULNERABILITIES	BEHAVIOR PATTERNS
- Sunlight weapons (invented)	• Silver mentioned but not emphas
- Regeneration (alow)	• Wooden stake through heart
- Weakesed by	• DESTOYED by sunlight (oral)
- Crystineide disruption	• Deamalic PATAs—
- Telapaphic network	• MUST be invited into homes
- Can enter any dwellings	• Feeds indiscrimately

STRATEGIC GOALS ACHIEVED:

1. Sunlight weakness (invented) enoures daytime sightings dismissed
2. Invitation requirement (false) explains home invasions as "proof"
3. Religious symbol effectiveness (false) prevents useful defensive mea-
4. Strategic antis heart netitad (noffective) ensures civilian attempts will
5. Romantic aristocratic portrayal makes reality seem too crude to match
6. Specific, elaborate "ruler" create expectation that any deviation proves "not a vampire"   RESULT:

AUTHORIZED: Edmund Weston, Duke of Weston
DATE: 18 August 1890   CLASSIFICATION

IN UMBRA LUCIS

The Duke stood, stretching. "Tomorrow, we'll go deeper—into their psychology, how they communicate. But tonight, rest. You've learned more about the Namtar than most field operatives know. And you've created a mythology that will hide them for generations."

He poured brandy for us all. "To the inversion. May fiction bury truth so deeply it can never be found."

Later, alone in my chamber, I spread the document on my desk and studied it by candlelight. On the left, truth—biological horrors engineered to replace humanity. On the right, fiction—a romantic monster bound by rules and vulnerable to common objects.

Which is crueler? The truth that would cause panic? Or the lie that leaves humanity defenseless against the real threat?

In Umbra Lucis.

I am in shadow now, thoroughly and completely. But perhaps others will remain in light because of it.

***

12th August, 1890

Weston Hall

This morning's session delved into Namtar psychology and social structure—or rather, how I must misrepresent it.

"The Namtar operate as a collective," Dr. Hartwell began. "Individual units retain autonomy, but they're connected through a crystalline network. Each one shares information instantaneously. When one learns something, all know it. They're like cells in a larger organism."

The Duke said, "Abandon this entirely. Make your vampire completely alone. No network. No collective. Perhaps he can create other vampires through his bite, but they're individuals, acting independently."

We covered their feeding patterns (strategic bloodline targeting versus random victim selection), their communication methods (telepathic network versus broken English with heavy accent), their powers (genuine superhuman abilities versus weakened mystical talents).

"Make him strong enough to be threatening," he advised, "but flawed enough to be defeated. Smart, but beatable. Your fictional heroes need a chance."

By afternoon, every aspect of Namtar nature had been inverted, simplified, or replaced with Gothic fantasy. Miss Marsh's notes grew into a comprehensive guide—a manual for creating the perfect lie.

"Resting places," Dr. Hartwell continued. "Namtar retreat to dark locations during daylight—dormant, conserving strength, protection. They're strongest in darkness."

"Make it necessary," the Duke said. "Your vampire must rest in his coffin during daylight. Make it a rule. Bind him to earth from his homeland—soil from Transylvania. Make daylight fatal, not just weakening. Extremely specific, completely false, but it gives heroes tactical advantage."

"Is he actually vulnerable during day rest?" I asked.

"Absolutely not. But your fictional vampire should be."

By evening, we had covered everything. Every real trait inverted or replaced. The complete mythology of Count Dracula, born not from folklore but from calculated misinformation.

The Duke showed me an older journal, leather-bound and water-stained. "1347," he said. "Black Death. One of ours suggested physicians blame rats and fleas rather than admit Namtar had infiltrated London. The lie held for centuries."

I read entries from a long-dead Arete member, wrestling with the same moral questions I now faced. His final entry: "The lie worked. I die knowing I saved thousands who will never know my name. In Umbra Lucis."

Seven hundred years later, his deception still protects us.

"You're doing remarkably well," Weston said at supper. "Many would have fled, unable to bear this charade."

"I confess, Your Grace, I still struggle with the morality."

"As you should. The day you stop questioning is the day you've lost your humanity." He paused. "But remember: every lie you tell, every false weakness you invent—it all protects millions who will sleep safely, never knowing what hunts in the dark. Is that not worth a troubled conscience?"

I had no answer.

After supper, I found a package in my chamber—a leather-bound journal, empty, with fine paper. A note from Miss Marsh:

"For your novel. Begin when ready. We've given you the tools. Now craft the weapon."

I opened to the first page and wrote:

DRACULA *By Bram Stoker*

Beneath it, in smaller letters where no one but I would see:

A Necessary Fiction

Tomorrow I return to London, to Florence, to the Lyceum. But I carry with me everything I need. Truth and lies, side by side. The inversion complete.

Now I must write the most important story of my life—knowing every word is false, hoping every lie might save someone.

***

1st September, 1890

London

I have been home three weeks now, settling back into the rhythms of the Lyceum. Irving is pleased with my renewed vigor—he thinks the holiday did me good. Florence is happy I'm focused on the new project. Neither knows the true nature of what I'm undertaking.

Tonight, after they've all gone to bed, I sit at my desk with the blank journal before me. The two-column document—Truth versus Fiction—lies beside it. The notes from Whitby. The materials from Weston Hall. Everything I need to begin... again.

A deep breath. I pray this treachery serves the greater good, for I am about to write the comfortable fiction that will blind the world to the true horror. What a dreadful responsibility.

I dip my pen and write:

Chapter 1 - JONATHAN HARKER'S JOURNAL

3 May. Bistritz.—Left Munich at 8:35 P.M., on 1st May, arriving at Vienna early next morning; should have arrived at 6:46, but train was an hour late. Buda-Pesth seems a wonderful place, from the glimpse which I got of it from the train and the little I could walk through the streets...

The words flow better this time. An innocent young solicitor, traveling to meet a foreign count. He has no idea what awaits him. Just as the people of Whitby had no idea – as most of humanity has no idea what the Westons fight.

I write for two hours before exhaustion forces me to stop. Five pages. The beginning of Jonathan Harker's journey. The beginning of my beautiful lie.

Tomorrow, the Lyceum demands my attention. But the nights—the nights are mine. The nights belong to Count Dracula.

***

12th October, 1890

London

Two months of writing. The first three chapters are complete. Jonathan has reached Castle Dracula, met the Count, begun to realize his danger. I write in the evenings after theatre work, and on Sunday afternoons when the Lyceum is dark.

Florence asked today what the novel was about. I told her it was a Gothic tale—a vampire story set in Transylvania and England. She laughed and said it sounded perfectly horrid.

"Will it be frightening?" she asked.

"I hope so," I said. "But entertainingly so. Like a ghost story told by firelight."

If she knew the real horror beneath the entertainment. If she knew I was writing a manual for public deception, sanctioned by an ancient order, designed to hide truths that would shatter her world.

But that's the point. She mustn't know. None of them must.

Irving asked to read some pages. I hesitated, but refusing entirely would seem odd—I've shared drafts with him before. I gave him the Whitby chapters, the atmospheric scenes of the Count's arrival. Safe enough, I thought. Gothic description.

Irving read them tonight. "Remarkable atmosphere, Bram. Almost as if you'd witnessed something terrible yourself." He paused, studying me. "The details are... unusually specific."

I said nothing.

"Well," he continued, returning the pages, "sometimes the best fiction comes from truths we cannot speak aloud." He smiled. "Theatre has taught me that much."

Did he know? Or was I reading too much into a casual remark?

I cannot let anyone else see the manuscript until it's complete. Until every false detail is in place, every invented weakness established, every misleading rule documented.

The work is slower than I hoped. The theatre consumes most of my energy. But I make progress. The Count is taking shape—aristocratic, menacing, seductive. Everything a Namtar is not.

***

14th October, 1890

London

Florence has become an unexpected asset. When I complained about needing authentic Victorian women's perspectives for Lucy and Mina, she offered to help—reading sections, suggesting dialogue, correcting my fumbling attempts at feminine interiority.

Today she made a suggestion that was pure genius: "Your vampire is too obviously foreign. He needs something that makes him seem almost English. Something that would allow him to blend into society. Perhaps... perfect manners? Aristocratic bearing? He should be able to attend the opera and pass completely unnoticed."

"Yes," I said slowly. "Yes, exactly that."

She smiled. "There. More frightening, isn't it? A monster that looks like a gentleman. We'd invite him into our drawing rooms without hesitation."

She's making my fictional vampire more convincing, which serves the Arete's purpose perfectly. Yet she has no idea she's helping to create strategic disinformation. The irony is not lost on me.

But more than that—she's talented. Her instincts are sharp. In another world, she might have been the writer in this family.

***

31st December, 1890

London

The year ends. Six months since my acceptance. The novel is under-way—perhaps a fifth complete, if I'm honest about the work ahead.

Tonight, as bells ring in the new year across London, I sit alone in my study reviewing what I've written. Jonathan's imprisonment in the castle. His growing horror. The three vampire women. Dracula's departure for England.

All fiction. Beautiful, detailed, convincing fiction.

I have created three female vampires who seduce and terrify. In reality, the Namtar are not divided by gender in any meaningful sense—they are weapons, not romantic Gothic phantoms. But my versions are creatures of desire and dread, perfectly suited for the story I must tell.

The two-column document sits beside my manuscript, constantly consulted. Every time I'm tempted to include a real detail, I stop. Check the fiction column. Write the lie instead.

It becomes easier with practice. The lying.

Florence is asleep upstairs. The house quiet. Outside, London celebrates. They don't know what I know. They don't carry what I carry.

Happy New Year. May the lies I write protect them all.

1891

1 **2th January, 1891**

London

The new year brings renewed focus. I've set myself a schedule: theatre work during the day, writing in the evenings and on Sundays. Florence has noticed my dedication, though she attributes it to artistic passion rather than strategic necessity.

"You're quite consumed by this vampire of yours," she observed last night.

"He consumes me," I replied, more truthfully than she knows.

I'm working on the early Transylvania chapters—Jonathan's imprisonment in Castle Dracula, his discovery of the Count's true nature. Every detail must establish the false mythology while maintaining Gothic atmosphere.

The Count climbs down the castle wall face-down, like a lizard. Dramatic, unsettling, memorable. Also: completely unlike how Namtar move. They don't need to climb walls—they can manipulate shadows, bend light, move through darkness itself.

But my Dracula must be physical, visible, bound by spatial limitations. Gothic monster, not quantum horror.

The distinction matters. Everything matters.

8th March, 1891

London

I have reached a difficult section—Lucy Westenra's transformation. In my story, she is sweet, innocent, destroyed by Dracula's curse. Her suffering must be romantic tragedy, not the agonizing horror Dr. Hartwell described in Whitby.

I write her as sleepwalking, drawn to the abbey by some mysterious compulsion. I write her growing pale, weak, beautiful in her decline. I write her three suitors desperate to save her, giving their blood in transfusions that cannot work because vampirism in my story is supernatural, not biological.

The reality: victims feel themselves changing. The cellular transformation is conscious, horrifying. They know what they're becoming and cannot stop it.

My fiction: Lucy dies peacefully, rises as a beautiful monster, feeds on children (shocking but literary), and is finally released by the stake through her heart.

The stake. Which doesn't actually work. But in my story, it's the key to salvation.

I finished the chapter tonight and felt ill. I have made horror into romance. Made torture into tragic beauty.

But isn't that the point? To make it so obviously fictional that reality seems impossible?

***

15th May, 1891

London

Irving commented today that I seem distracted. He's not wrong—my mind constantly returns to the manuscript. Even during rehearsals, I'm mentally drafting Van Helsing's speeches or refining Lucy's transformation scene.

"This novel has you in its grip," Irving said. "Is it that compelling?"

"It must be," I told him. "It must be compelling enough that people believe every word."

He laughed, thinking I meant literary merit. I meant strategic effectiveness.

I'm working on the middle section now—Lucy's slow decline, her sleepwalking, her mysterious illness. The doctors cannot help her because they don't understand what she faces.

Just like the real doctors in Whitby couldn't help their patients because they didn't know about Namtar.

But in my version, there's an answer. Van Helsing knows. Van Helsing has the ancient wisdom (that I'm inventing). Van Helsing can fight back with garlic, crosses, holy water.

All useless against real Namtar. But readers won't know that.

"Your Count Dracula," Irving mused, "follows rules very different from traditional folklore. Deliberate inversions, almost." He tapped the manuscript. "One might think you're teaching readers to look for the wrong monster."

"One might," I said carefully.

Irving smiled. "Good. The best stories are the useful ones."

***

15th June, 1891

Weston Hall

I returned to Sussex for the first time since August, carrying my manuscript—the first half, roughly complete. The Duke, Dr. Hartwell, and Miss Marsh reviewed it over two days.

"Excellent," the Duke pronounced. "You've captured the Gothic atmosphere while systematically inverting every truth. Lucy's transformation is perfect—romantic, tragic, nothing like the real horror."

Dr. Hartwell pointed to a scene. "Here, where Van Helsing explains vampire lore. This is your opportunity to establish the false rules with authority. Make him absolutely confident. Readers will believe him because he's the expert."

"Van Helsing is based partly on you," I told Miss Marsh. "His scholarly nature, his certainty."

She smiled. "Then make him very certain indeed. The more authoritative the lie, the more believable it becomes."

Thomas Weston—the Duke's son, now seventeen—asked to meet me. He's tall, serious, with his father's sharp eyes. Already trained in combat, already a veteran of his first Namtar encounter.

"Thank you," he said quietly. "For doing this. My father told me what you're creating. A shield we can hide behind for generations."

"I hope so," I said.

"You will," he replied with certainty beyond his years. "My father has already begun... preparing the ground. Quietly spreading the folklore you're documenting. When your book is published, people will recognize the 'ancient traditions' you've written about. They'll think you're simply recording what's always been known."

His words both encouraged and unsettled me. The Duke's network is already planting seeds—spreading the false mythology through whispers, through scholarly articles, through carefully placed 'folklore' references. By the time my book appears, readers will think I'm confirming ancient lore, not inventing it.

The Duke walked me through the gardens before I departed.

"Your progress is remarkable. Continue. We have time—this is not a race. Better to do it thoroughly than quickly."

"It may take years," I warned.

"Good," he said. "The best lies are carefully constructed. Take the time you need."

***

22nd August, 1891

London

Summer heat torments London. The theatre is stifling. My study is barely cooler.

Today I crafted the scene where Lucy, now undead, feeds on children in Hampstead. It's meant to be shocking—the pure woman corrupted into a predator of innocents. Victorian morality play about the dangers of female sexuality.

But beneath the metaphor lies strategic purpose: show that vampires can be defeated. That stakes work. That the threat can be eliminated through known methods.

Give readers hope. Give them weapons (that don't work). Give them the illusion of control.

Florence read this section and pronounced it "deliciously horrible." She asked if I'd based Lucy on anyone.

"Composite of several women I've known," I lied. Lucy is based on Mary Thornton. On the child. On all twelve Whitby victims whose real transformations were far more terrible than anything I could publish.

I made their horror Gothic. Made their suffering tragic. Made their deaths meaningful.

It's the best I can do for them.

***

20th September, 1891

London

Today I created Professor Abraham Van Helsing. The vampire expert. The authority on "ancient lore" that I'm inventing as I write.

Van Helsing will be Dutch—foreign, scholarly, credible. He will explain all the rules with utter confidence: garlic repels vampires, crosses burn them, sunlight destroys them, stakes through the heart kill them, they cannot cross running water, they must be invited into homes.

Every word he speaks will be false. But spoken with such authority that readers will believe.

Miss Marsh's influence is clear in his character—the meticulous note-taking, the reference to ancient texts, the absolute certainty in his knowledge. But I've made him warmer than Adelaide, more accessible. A figure readers will trust implicitly.

He will be the voice of expertise. And every word of his expertise will be calculated misinformation.

Florence read a few pages tonight—the first time I've let anyone see the manuscript. She pronounced Van Helsing "wonderfully wise and reassuring."

Exactly as intended.

***

30th October, 1891

London

All Hallows Eve tomorrow. Appropriate timing—I'm writing the scene where the vampire hunters stake Lucy, releasing her soul—the destruction of Lucy, undead. In my version, Arthur Holmwood drives the wooden stake through her heart while Van Helsing reads prayers. She writhes, cries out, then finds peace. Her face returns to its living beauty. Her soul is saved.

Romantic. Tragic. Cathartic.

The reality: wooden stakes don't work on Namtar. Only silver and beheading. But I've made the stake the primary weapon. Easily available. Simple to understand. Completely ineffective.

Perfect misinformation.

Dr. Hartwell would approve. In fact, I've sent him this chapter for review. He'll verify that every detail contradicts reality effectively.

This is my life now—crafting lies, checking them for accuracy of inaccuracy, ensuring each fiction is convincing enough to bury truth.

But I cannot write that. Cannot give readers the truth.

So I give them this—a beautiful lie wrapped in Gothic prose and Victorian morality.

Irving wants to read the manuscript soon. I'm running out of excuses. Perhaps I'll show him selected chapters—the ones that seem purely literary, nothing that reveals the strategic intent.

***

30th November, 1891

London

A year since I truly committed to this work. The novel is perhaps half complete now—slower than I'd like, but thorough. Every detail checked against the two-column document. Every false rule established with care.

Irving has been patient with my divided attention. The Lyceum prospers, but I know my heart is elsewhere these days. In Transylvania with my fictional Count. In Whitby with my doomed Lucy. In London with my brave vampire hunters.

Brave, fictional vampire hunters who will succeed because I give them weapons that don't actually work.

I had doubts again tonight. Strong ones. Is this right? Creating such an elaborate deception?

But then I remembered the photographs from Whitby.

If my lie saves even one person from that fate—if my fiction prevents even one panic, one witch hunt, one innocent person accused—isn't it worth this troubled conscience?

I must believe it is. Because I cannot stop now.

1892

20th January, 1892

London

New year, new complications. Irving insists on reading the manuscript. I've given him the first third—Jonathan's journey, the castle, Dracula's arrival in England, Lucy's transformation.

He read it over three days and pronounced it "magnificent, though perhaps too cerebral for popular taste."

Too cerebral. If only he knew.

"Your Count is fascinating," Irving said. "Aristocratic, yes, but also foreign, dangerous. He represents everything Victorian England fears about continental influence."

"Exactly," I said, letting him believe the social commentary is the point.

It IS a point—just not the main one. The main point being: here are the rules. Memorize them. Spread them. Believe them.

So when real Namtar appear, everyone will say: "But that's not how vampires work."

***

14th February, 1892

London

The novel progresses. Lucy is dead and staked. Mina Harker is now Dracula's target. The hunters are in pursuit. The mythology is complete and consistent throughout—every false rule established, every invented weakness documented, every romantic notion firmly in place.

Florence commented yesterday that I seem haunted by this project. She's not wrong. I am haunted—by what I know, by what I'm creating, by the weight of this deception.

***

25th April, 1892

London

"You're more invested in this fictional Count than in your real family," Florence said over dinner.

An unfair accusation, though not entirely wrong. I AM invested beyond what seems rational for a novel.

"It's important work," I said.

"It's a Gothic entertainment," she countered. "Why does it consume you so?"

I wanted to tell her. God, how I wanted to explain: This "entertainment" will protect millions. This "fiction" is actually the most important work I've ever done. This "obsession" serves a purpose she can't imagine.

But I stayed silent. Because telling her would defeat the entire purpose.

"I'll be finished soon," I promised. A lie—I have years of work ahead.

She accepted it, though I could see doubt in her eyes.

***

10th May, 1892

London

Something remarkable happened today. A woman came to the Lyceum seeking me—introduced by one of the Duke's connections. Her husband died in the Whitby incident of 1885. She wanted to thank me.

"His Grace told me you're writing something," she said carefully. "Something that will help people... understand. Or rather, not understand. If you follow my meaning."

I invited her to my office.

"My William was one of the twelve," she said quietly. "The doctors told me it was illness. Contamination. I knew better—I saw what happened to him those last days. But I still accepted their lie. Do you understand, Mr. Stoker? Sometimes a lie is a mercy."

"I do understand," I said.

"His Grace says your book will make it so people don't have to face what I faced. They'll have a story—a safe story—to believe instead. That's a gift, sir. A kindness to those who come after."

After she left, I wept. The first time since beginning this work that I've allowed myself tears.

She's right. Sometimes a lie is a mercy. Sometimes fiction protects better than truth.

I returned to the manuscript with renewed purpose.

***

15th June, 1892

London

Florence came into my study this evening while I was working. I didn't hear her enter—too focused on cross-referencing the false rules with Dr. Hartwell's notes.

"Abraham," she said quietly, and I nearly knocked the ink bottle over in my haste to cover the documents.

She picked up a page from the manuscript. "'The vampire cannot cross running water'—but here in your research notes"—she gestured to the Arete documents I'd failed to conceal—"it says 'specimen crossed Thames without difficulty, 1885.' Which is correct?"

My throat went dry. "The first. The novel version. The notes are... earlier theories. Discarded."

"Discarded." She studied my face. "You're lying to me. You've been lying for months. I don't know about what, but I know my husband."

"Florence—"

"I won't press. Clearly you cannot tell me." She set the page down carefully. "But whatever this truly is—whatever you're involved in—please be careful. You're not merely a writer anymore, are you? You're something else. And it frightens me."

After she left, I locked everything away properly. She's more perceptive than I gave her credit for. The Duke warned me: the burden of secrecy extends to those we love. Sometimes protecting them means letting them believe we've simply grown distant.

But Florence deserves better than that.

***

12th July, 1892

London

Working on Mina's character today. She must be the moral center—intelligent, brave, faithful. The pure woman who is partially corrupted but fights back, saved by love and friendship.

Victorian readers will appreciate her. She embodies proper womanhood while also showing modern independence—she types Jonathan's journal entries, she joins the hunt, she faces danger.

But her real purpose: demonstrate that vampirism can be resisted. That partial infection can be fought. That there's hope even after the vampire's bite.

False hope, regarding real Namtar. Once the pathogen takes hold, transformation is inevitable. There is no fighting it through willpower or faith.

But Mina will fight it. And win. Because my readers need to believe it's possible.

I'm crafting hopeful lies. Perhaps the kindest kind.

***

8th October, 1892

London

I'm writing Van Helsing's long exposition tonight—his explanation of vampire lore to the other hunters. Pages of false information delivered with absolute authority.

"The vampire, he cannot die by the mere passing of time; he can flourish when he can fatten on the blood of the living..."

True enough. They don't age.

"...he can, within his range, direct the elements: the storm, the fog, the thunder..."

Partially true—they can manipulate shadow and darkness, which might appear as controlling weather.

"...he can command all the meaner things: the rat, and the owl, and the bat..."

False. They have no such power.

"...he can appear at will when and where and in any of the forms that are to him..."

False. They cannot shapeshift.

"...he cannot flourish without this diet of blood; he throws no shadow; he make in the mirror no reflect..."

All false.

Van Helsing speaks with such certainty. Such scholarly authority. And every certainty is a carefully constructed lie.

The best lies contain kernels of truth. Enough to seem credible. And enough to be believed.

***

22nd November, 1892

London

A most unsettling night at the theatre. I found myself standing near two society ladies who, astonishingly, began speculating aloud about the creature in question.

"I find the idea of them quite tragic, don't you, Mrs. Albright?" said the first, stirring her tea. "To be sensitive to silver, but otherwise so terribly human. It makes one pity them." "Pity, perhaps, but they can't be invited everywhere," the other replied sharply. "They are creatures of the *night*, dear. They can't merely stride about in the full sun like a normal gentleman."

I had to clench my jaw to maintain a neutral expression. These limitations—the silver sensitivity, the aversion to bright daylight—were fabrications I had introduced only last month to make the beast more palatable and less supernatural. And yet, here they are, the elegant ladies of London, discussing them as settled, ancient truths.

The Duke's propagandists are frighteningly efficient. They've managed to turn my convenient lie into drawing-room gossip. The speed at which the new mythology is supplanting the old is terrifying.

I nearly laughed. They were quoting rules I haven't even published yet—rules that have somehow leaked into general conversation, probably through the Duke's network spreading "folklore."

The mythology is taking root before the book is complete. Cultural osmosis. People absorbing these falsehoods as ancient wisdom.

It's working. God help me, it's actually working.

***

28th December, 1892

London

Christmas was quiet. Florence's family visited. Everyone jolly, festive, blissfully ignorant.

I received a card from the Duke—nothing written inside except the crest and "In Umbra Lucis." No need for more. We understand each other.

People like him. Bloodline sensitives. Those who carry the genetic markers that make them both able to fight Namtar and vulnerable to being targeted by them.

If the public knew about bloodline sensitives, they'd hunt them. Think them contaminated, corrupted, dangerous.

So we hide them behind layers of fiction. Make vampirism about random bites, not genetic predisposition. Make it something that could happen to anyone, not something concentrated in specific families.

His son, Thomas and others like him will live safer because of my lies.

That has to be enough.

1893

1 **5th January, 1893**

London

Burned three pages today. Wrote them, read them, realized they were too close to truth. Burned them. Started over with better lies.

My wastepaper basket fills with honesty. My manuscript fills with mythology.

That's the work.

All I can do is continue. Trust the Duke's thousand years of experience. Trust that those who've fought this war longer than my language has existed know better than I do.

But the question torments me: betraying or protecting?

Perhaps both. Perhaps that's what *In Umbra Lucis* truly means.

***

5th March, 1893

London

I'm writing the chase sequence now—Dracula fleeing back to Transylvania, the heroes in pursuit. Racing against time, against the sunset, against the Count's dark powers.

It must be exciting. Breathless. The climax everything builds toward.

But also: it must show that all vampires CAN be defeated. That ordinary men with courage and the right knowledge (false knowledge, but they don't know that) can triumph over supernatural evil.

Hope. I'm writing hope into every page.

False hope. But hope nonetheless.

***

3rd April, 1893

Weston Hall

Returned to Sussex for consultation. I've been away too long—nearly two years since my last visit. Weston is grayer, more worn. The war takes its toll on everyone.

Young Thomas is now nineteen, already a full Arete operative. He's killed three Namtar scouts in the past year, coordinating with European operations. His father's pride and fear are equally evident.

"Every generation," the Duke said quietly, watching his son train in the courtyard. "Every generation, we send our children to fight monsters. Your book, Mr. Stoker—it won't save my son. He'll still face the real threats. But perhaps it will save someone else's child from being caught in the crossfire of a public panic."

He showed me old documents again—the William the Conqueror materials, the Viking accounts, the Norman invasion. Context for perseverance.

"Nine hundred years," he said. "My family has held this responsibility for nine hundred years. What are seven years of writing compared to that? Please take the time you need to do it right."

I returned to London recommitted. The long view. Generations. This is bigger than my immediate comfort.

***

18th June, 1893

London

Extraordinary letter arrived today. A folklore scholar named William Fielding wrote asking about my research into vampire legends. Word has spread that I'm writing "an extensively researched vampire novel."

He wants to know my sources. Particularly regarding the sunlight weakness, which he claims not to find in Eastern European folklore.

Because I invented it, Mr. Fielding. Because there IS no ancient source.

I wrote back vaguely about "various texts, compiled over years of study" and "oral traditions documented during travels." Let him think I have secret sources I won't share.

The Duke will be pleased—even before publication, the mythology begins to take on an air of scholarly authenticity.

Fielding believes I'm revealing ancient truths. In reality, I'm creating modern lies.

But if scholars like him believe it, others will too.

***

18th July, 1893

Scotland

A "research trip" to the Highlands—though in reality, visiting an Arete containment facility. The Duke arranged it, thinking I should see more of their operations.

The facility is hidden in a remote glen, disguised as a private estate. Inside, I saw technology I barely comprehend—crystal-based detection equipment, weapons designed specifically for Namtar combat, preserved specimens from centuries past.

They showed me the site of an 1891 incident—a village where two Namtar scouts attacked before being contained. Local records attribute the deaths to influenza. The truth is locked in Arete archives.

I took copious notes on Scottish legends—folklore I can incorporate. Local color for the novel. People died here, and the world never knew.

***

19th July, 1893

Scotland - Arete Facility

Dr. Hartwell showed me something today that will haunt me far longer than any preserved specimen.

A young woman, twenty-four years old, who'd been partially infected before being saved. The pathogen removed through experimental crystal frequency treatment—technology still being perfected.

She was alive. But changed. Haunted. She could sense Namtar approaching now—useful for the Arete, they said. An early warning system. But she also suffered nightmares, flashbacks, phantom sensations of the transformation that almost happened.

"We saved her," Dr. Hartwell said quietly. "But we couldn't save who she was before."

She wouldn't meet my eyes. Couldn't bear to be in the same room with the specimens. Flinched at shadows.

This is what partial infection looks like when caught early. This is the best-case scenario.

In my novel, Mina will be saved cleanly. Completely. She'll bear only a small scar—a mark of what she survived, but fundamentally unchanged. Still herself. Still whole.

The reality is harsher. More cruel.

It is not possible to write that reality. So I write the hope instead.

***

15th November, 1893

London

The climax is complete. Jonathan and Quincey attack Dracula as the sun sets—Jonathan slashing the Count's throat while Quincey drives his knife into the heart. Dracula crumbles to dust. Quincey dies from his wounds but dies a hero.

Dramatic. Satisfying. Clear victory over evil.

Also: completely misleading about how to actually kill Namtar.

Throat slashing: ineffective. Heart stabbing: ineffective. The sun touching them at the moment of death: meaningless.

Only beheading severs the crystalline network permanently. Only silver slows their regeneration. Everything else is theatre.

But my readers won't know that. They'll learn Jonathan and Quincey's methods. They'll think THAT'S how you kill vampires.

And if they ever face a real Namtar? They'll be defensively useless.

But they'll also likely not believe they're facing a real threat. Because it won't match the Count's profile.

***

3rd December, 1893 *London*

Heart still racing. Close call this morning.

Florence reading the Cornwall Chronicle over breakfast. "How odd," she said. "Listen to this: 'Mysterious deaths in Cornwall continue to baffle authorities. Twelve victims over three weeks, all showing similar symptoms of progressive weakness and pallor. Local physician notes unusual marks on victims' throats but dismisses supernatural explanations.'"

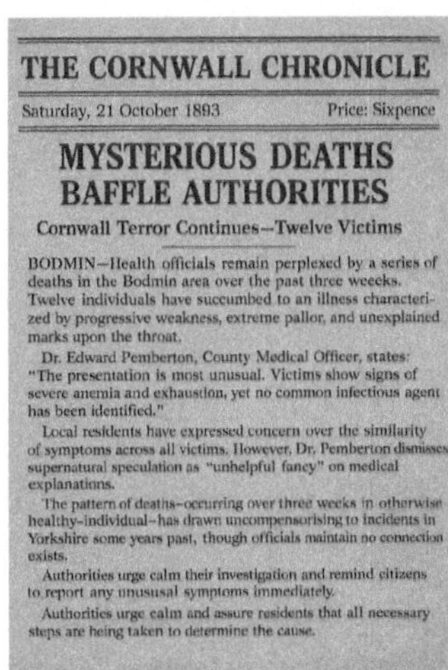

THE CORNWALL CHRONICLE

Saturday, 21 October 1893   Price: Sixpence

MYSTERIOUS DEATHS BAFFLE AUTHORITIES

Cornwall Terror Continues—Twelve Victims

BODMIN—Health officials remain perplexed by a series of deaths in the Bodmin area over the past three weeeks. Twelve individuals have succumbed to an illness characterized by progressive weakness, extreme pallor, and unexplained marks upon the throat.

Dr. Edward Pemberton, County Medical Officer, states: "The presentation is most unusual. Victims show signs of severe anemia and exhaustion, yet no common infectious agent has been identified."

Local residents have expressed concern over the similarity of symptoms across all victims. However, Dr. Pemberton dismisses supernatural speculation as "unhelpful fancy" on medical explanations.

The pattern of deaths—occurring over three weeks in otherwise healthy-individual—has drawn uncompensorising to incidents in Yorkshire some years past, though officials maintain no connection exists.

Authorities urge calm their investigation and remind citizens to report any unususal symptoms immediately.

Authorities urge calm and assure residents that all necessary steps are being taken to determine the cause.

Cornwall Chronicle

She looked up. "Twelve victims. Throat marks. Exactly like in your novel. You're quite prescient, Abraham. Or perhaps you read about Cornwall incidents and used them for inspiration?"

"Pure coincidence," I managed. "Gothic fiction uses similar tropes."

"Mm." She returned to the paper. "Though the timeline is interesting. These deaths began in October. You finished that section of Dracula in... when? September?"

"August," I said, then cursed myself. Why volunteer precision?

"So you wrote about throat marks and mysterious deaths in August, and they appear in Cornwall in October." She folded the paper. "Quite the coincidence indeed."

She left for her morning calls. I immediately sent telegram to Weston Hall: CORNWALL COVERAGE TOO DETAILED STOP
SUGGESTS PATTERN STOP CONTAIN STORY

The Duke's reply came within hours: ALREADY HANDLED
STOP NO FURTHER COVERAGE STOP YOUR WIFE PER-
CEPTIVE STOP CAREFUL

How careful must I be in my own home?

TELEGRAM

TO: WESTON HALL SUSSEX
FROM: A. STOKER LONDON
DATE: 3 DECEMBER 1893

CORNWALL COVERAGE
TOO DETAILED STOP
SUGGESTS PATTERN
CONTAIN STORY
STOP
A. STOKER

A. STOKER

TELEGRAM

TO: A STOKER LONDON
FROM: WESTON HALL SUSSEX
DATE: 3 DECEMBER 1893

ALREADY HANDLED STOP

NO FURTHER COVERAGE
STOP

YOUR WIFE PERCEPTIVE
STOP

CAREFUL STOP

W

1894

5th January, 1894

London

I have a complete draft. Rough, needing revision, but complete from Jonathan's journey to Dracula's destruction.

This morning I wrote "THE END" and sat staring at the words for ten minutes.

Done. The seven-year lie complete in its first form.

But it's rough. Very rough. Pacing issues. Inconsistencies. Places where I've accidentally included true details that must be changed.

The entire mythology is in place:

Vampires are undead, cursed

They drink blood for   sustenance

Sunlight destroys them

Crosses and holy water repel   them

Garlic deters them

They cannot cross running   water

They must be invited into   homes

Wooden stakes through the heart kill them

They cast no reflection

They can transform into wolves, bats, mist

Every single detail is false. Every weakness invented. Every rule designed to make the truth unrecognizable.

The real work begins now: revision. Making it clean, consistent, compelling. Making sure every false rule is established clearly. Making sure no truth accidentally slips through.

I sent word to Weston Hall: "First draft complete. Ready for review."

The Duke replied within two days: "Excellent. Bring it yourself. We'll review together. - W"

February, then. I'll return to Sussex in February with the manuscript. Let the Arete team examine every page.

Let them tell me what must change to make the lie perfect.

***

16th February, 1894

Weston Hall

Three days at Weston Hall. Weston, Dr. Hartwell, Miss Marsh, and Thomas all reviewing the manuscript. Each reading with different focus.

The Duke: Strategic effectiveness. Does it accomplish the mission?

Dr. Hartwell: Biological accuracy of the inaccuracies. Are the lies effective?

Miss Marsh: Consistency. Are the false rules maintained throughout?

Thomas: Reader perspective. Would someone his age believe it?

They made extensive notes. Hundreds of small adjustments. A few larger changes.

Dr. Hartwell: "Chapter 18—the blood transfusion scene reads too scientifically accurate. Make it more mystical. We want people thinking in terms of supernatural exchange, not medical procedure. Modern medicine might eventually allow people to test your claims."

Miss Marsh: "Throughout—excellent consistency in false rules. But consider adding more Christian symbolism. The more you tie vampirism to concepts of sin and redemption, the more it seems allegorical rather than literal."

Thomas: "Lucy's transformation is perfect. She's sympathetic, her death is tragic, and the stake through her heart is clear and memorable. This will become the iconic vampire death scene."

The Duke: "Well done overall. However, I suggest softening Dracula's intelligence slightly. Make him cunning but not quite as strategic as a true Namtar. Make him beatable through cleverness, not only force. Give readers hope they could actually fight back if needed."

We also discussed the Munich chapter—Jonathan's encounter before reaching Transylvania. He felt it showed too much supernatural danger in Western Europe, too close to home.

"Keep the horror focused in Transylvania," he advised. "Make the threat foreign, distant, exotic. Even though Namtar are everywhere—including London—readers should think of vampires as Eastern European phenomenon. Makes it feel less immediate."

I'm taking notes on all their feedback. The revision will take months.

But we're close. So close.

***

18th March, 1894

London - Lyceum Theatre

Irving called me into his office this afternoon. He had the manuscript—the latest section—spread across his desk.

"This bit about the Count climbing down the castle wall," he said. "Head-first, like a lizard. Quite disturbing image. Where'd you get it?"

"Imagination," I said.

"Really? Because I could swear... There was a backstage incident, wasn't there? Years ago, before you joined us. Stagehand claimed he saw someone climbing the exterior wall at night. Impossible height. Moved all wrong, he said. Head-first down the brickwork."

My blood ran cold. "I don't recall that."

"No? Well, he was drunk, probably. Fired for drinking on the job. But the image stayed with me." Irving tapped the page. "And here it is in your novel. Quite specific. Almost as if you'd seen it yourself."

"Pure invention," I insisted. "Common Gothic imagery—unnatural movement, violation of natural law."

"Of course." But his eyes studied me. "Though you've been remarkably specific about other details too. The way the Count drinks—not only blood, but the manner of it. The transformation process. The rules about invitations and thresholds. It all feels very... researched. As if you had access to some source material I don't know about."

"Only folklore and legend."

"Mm." He handed back the pages. "Well, it's effective. Unsettlingly so. Sometimes I wonder if you've tapped into something real, Stoker. Something you're not telling me."

He smiled, but it didn't reach his eyes.

After leaving his office, hands shaking, I realized: the Lyceum incident was real. Eighteen years ago. A Namtar scout, eliminated by Arete before it could establish a nest. The drunk stagehand saw it climbing.

And I'd used that exact image without thinking. Drew from the Arete reports I'd read. Irving is too clever, too observant. He suspects something.

Must be more careful. Cannot let the truth bleed through.

***

4th May, 1894

London

Munich chapter is cut. The publisher agreed it slowed the pace—they wanted readers to reach Castle Dracula faster. But I think the Duke's reasoning was equally valid: keep the threat distant.

I've saved the cut chapter. Perhaps someday, after I'm gone, it can be published separately. By then, the mythology will be too well-established to shake. The cut chapter won't undermine the main work.

But for now, it's removed. First chapter begins with Jonathan's journal from Bistritz, already well into his journey.

Straight to Transylvania. Straight to the foreign threat. Nothing to suggest supernatural danger lurks in Munich, London, or anywhere else civilized Victorians might travel.

Strategic editing. Everything is strategy now.

***

12th June, 1894

Weston Hall

Thomas Weston read the manuscript. He's now twenty, veteran of numerous operations, and his perspective proved invaluable.

"This will save lives," he said with certainty. "Not because it kills Namtar—we'll still do that. But because when civilians encounter evidence of them, they'll compare it to your book and dismiss it. 'Real vampires don't act like this,' they'll say. And they'll be right—real Namtar don't act like your Dracula at all."

We walked the grounds together. He showed me scars from a fight in Dover last month—a Namtar scout trying to infiltrate from France. Silver blade across his ribs, nearly died.

"I don't fear death," he said. "I fear what happens if we fail. If people learn the truth before they're ready. The panic. The chaos. Your book prevents that. It's a kindness, Mr. Stoker."

His father's son. Same burden, same duty, same terrible knowledge.

He'll have children someday. Train them as he was trained. Pass the duty forward.

And my book will help protect them all.

***

28th August, 1894

London

The Duke's son brought his fiancée to meet his father. A young woman named Catherine, from another bloodline sensitive family—the match carefully arranged, of course. Their children will carry both genetic lines.

"We're continuing the work begun with William the Conqueror," the Duke told me over brandy while Thomas and Catherine walked the gardens. "Bloodline breeding. Creating the next generation of guardians."

"Does she know?" I asked. "What she's marrying into?"

"She knows her family history. She knows she's bloodline sensitive. She knows the duty." He paused. "But she loves Thomas regardless. Sometimes love and duty align."

I thought of Florence. She doesn't know. Can never know. Our marriage is simply love, no strategic purpose behind it.

"Do you ever wish you'd been able to choose freely?" I asked.

"Every day," the Duke said quietly. "And never. The burden is terrible. But abandoning it would be worse."

In Umbra Lucis.

Some of us carry the weight by choice. Some by birth. All for the same purpose.

***

2nd November, 1894

London

Working late into the night. The revisions are nearly complete. Every note from the Arete team addressed. Every false rule sharpened. Every strategic element refined.

Van Helsing's exposition is now longer, more detailed. He explains vampire lore with even more certainty. Cites ancient texts (that don't exist). References cases he's studied (that never happened).

The authority of the expert sells the lie. Readers will trust him completely.

Because I've made him trustworthy. Scholarly. Brave. Right about everything (that's wrong).

Florence caught me muttering Van Helsing's lines while working. "Are you rehearsing?" she asked.

"In a way," I said. Rehearsing lies until they sound like truth.

Irving would be proud of the performance. Method acting taken to its extreme.

I'm not just writing a character. I'm embodying the deception.

***

8th November, 1894

London

The revision process is thorough but satisfying. The novel is taking its final shape—every scene polished, every false detail sharpened, every character refined.

Florence has been very patient, though she doesn't understand it. How could she? She thinks I'm writing Gothic entertainment. She's not entirely wrong—it will be entertaining. But its true purpose is something she can never know.

Irving grows impatient for me to finish so I can return full attention to the Lyceum. Soon, I promise. Soon.

The lies are nearly complete.

***

24th December, 1894

London

Noel asked me about my book today. He's eight now, old enough to be curious about his father's work.

"Papa, is your book about real monsters?"

"No, son. Make-believe monsters. For entertainment."

"But you have drawings. In your study. I saw them when I wasn't supposed to be in there." He looked guilty. "Sorry. But the drawings... they didn't look make-believe. They looked like... like scientific drawings. With measurements and notes."

Florence looked up sharply from her sewing.

"Anatomical studies," I said quickly. "To make the fiction more believable. Artists' reference materials."

"Oh." He seemed satisfied. "Can I see the book when it's published?"

"When you're older, perhaps. It's rather frightening."

After he went to bed, Florence spoke quietly: "He's right, you know. Those drawings in your study don't look like reference materials. They look like medical illustrations. Of something real."

"Florence—"

"I'm not asking. I stopped asking." She returned to her sewing. "But perhaps lock your study. Our son is curious, and you're careless."

She's right. I've become too comfortable. Too complacent. Even my eight-year-old son can see the truth bleeding through the fiction.

Tomorrow I lock everything away properly. The Duke's documents, the Arete reports, all of it. No more leaving evidence where innocent eyes might find it.

In protecting the world from truth, I nearly exposed my own family to it.

1895

5 **th January, 1895**

London

Six years since recruitment. The second complete draft is finished—cleaner, stronger, more consistent than the first. Every false rule is now firmly established. Every invented weakness clearly documented.

I reread the entire manuscript over the past three days, experiencing it as a fresh reader might. And I confess: even knowing every word is a lie, I found myself believing it. The authority of Van Helsing's exposition, the specificity of the rules, the consistency throughout—it all feels authentic.

If I can convince myself, knowing the truth, imagine how persuasive it will be to readers who don't know.

That's both comforting and terrifying.

Irving read the revised manuscript and declared it "your finest work yet, Bram. Dark, unsettling, but ultimately hopeful. The triumph of good over evil through knowledge and courage."

Knowledge. Courage. If he only knew how deliberately I'd crafted false knowledge to give readers false courage.

But that false courage might save their lives by making them dismiss real threats as impossible.

Layers upon layers of untruths, all serving the same purpose.

***

3rd February, 1895

London

Second complete draft finished. I've adjusted pacing, tightened the plot, added more Victorian moral dimension as Miss Marsh suggested. The novel is stronger for it.

Mina Harker has become the moral center—the pure woman partially corrupted, fighting against darkness, ultimately saved by her friends' devotion and her own strength. Victorian readers will appreciate the religious allegory.

They won't realize the allegory hides truth far more disturbing than any gothic fantasy.

***

22nd April, 1895

London

Strange encounter today. I was at the British Library researching minor details for final revisions when I met a young scholar studying European folklore. He asked what I was working on.

"A novel about vampires," I said carefully.

His face lit up. "How fascinating! Have you encountered the traditions about sunlight being fatal to them? And the requirement that they be invited into dwellings? Those elements appear across multiple cultures, though documentation is scarce."

They don't appear across multiple cultures. I made them up.

But I nodded sagely. "Yes, those traditions are quite consistent, though the sources are difficult to track."

"Exactly!" he said enthusiastically. "I've been trying to find primary sources for years. The oral traditions must predate written records by centuries."

I let him believe it. Let him think he'd confirmed authentic folklore rather than absorbing planted misinformation that the Duke's network has been spreading.

The mythology takes root in academic circles before the book is even published. Perfect.

***

15th May, 1895

London

Five years since Whitby. Five years since I stood on those cliffs and learned the truth. Half a decade of carrying this secret, crafting this lie.

The novel is substantially complete. Final polish needed, but the work is essentially done. Every false rule in place. Every invented weakness documented. Every element designed to obscure truth.

I reread it today, start to finish, imagining a reader discovering it fresh. Would they believe vampires could be real? Would they find the rules convincing?

Yes. I think they would. And that's precisely the problem—or the solution, depending on perspective.

Convincing enough to be believed. False enough to hide truth.

Perfect.

***

14th July, 1895

London

Summer heat is oppressive. The theatre is unbearable. But I press on with final polishing.

Today I refined the scene where Mina, partially infected by Dracula's blood, feels his presence across distance. She can sense where he is, what he's feeling. The psychic connection between vampire and victim.

This part is actually somewhat true—Namtar do have a network connection. But it works completely differently than I've portrayed. It's not individual psychic bonds but a collective consciousness through crystalline pathways.

I've made it personal, romantic, mystical. Made it about Dracula's specific bite creating a unique connection with Mina.

False enough to mislead while close enough to feel authentic. The best lies always contain that kernel of truth.

***

9th September, 1895

Weston Hall

Adelaide Marsh's final review. She checked every supernatural detail against the truth, ensuring no accidental facts slipped through.

"Perfect disinformation," she pronounced. "I could not have done better myself."

She showed me something curious—her own annotated copy of the manuscript. Two versions: one for publication, one for Arete archives with marginal notes explaining what each fictional element actually conceals.

"This will be kept in the Deep Archives," she said. "So future generations understand what you did. How you protected humanity with carefully constructed lies."

The archive copy will survive long after I'm gone. Long after everyone who knows the truth has died. Future Arete warriors will study it, understanding how fiction can be weaponized.

I've created something that will outlast me.

***

1st October, 1895

London

Extraordinary news. Adelaide Marsh visited London—rare for her to leave Weston Hall. She brought two manuscripts: mine, and her own annotated copy.

Her copy contains marginal notes throughout explaining the truth behind each fiction. A key to decode the lies.

"This will be sealed in the Deep Archives," she explained over tea in my study. "So future generations of Arete understand what was done and why. Your published novel will be the public version. This annotated manuscript will be the true record."

She showed me some of her notes:

"Page 47: Stoker writes that vampires cannot cross running water. Truth: Namtar have no such limitation. Strategic purpose: Makes readers think rivers and streams provide protection. May reduce panic if incidents occur near water."

"Page 193: Stoker describes wooden stake through heart as fatal. Truth: Wood is ineffective. Only beheading kills permanently. Strategic purpose: Gives public a 'weapon' that creates false sense of security while ensuring they won't accidentally discover effective methods."

Page after page. Truth beside fiction. The Rosetta Stone of my fabrication.

"Will anyone ever read this?" I asked.

"Perhaps," she said. "If the Namtar threat is ever fully eliminated. If humanity becomes ready for truth. But more likely, it will remain forever in the archives. A secret history of a secret war."

After she left, I felt oddly validated. Someone will know. Someday. Even if it's centuries from now, someone will understand what I truly did.

That has to be enough.

***

28th November, 1895

London

Christmas approaching but the manuscript demands attention. Every detail matters. Every word carries weight.

I refined Renfield's character today—the madman who serves Dracula, who eats living creatures to absorb their life force. He's meant to be tragic, pitiable, a warning about the dangers of seeking immortality through dark means.

But he also serves a strategic purpose: he shows that serving vampires leads to madness, degradation, death. Discourages anyone who might be tempted to seek out such creatures for promised power.

Even Renfield, who seems like a minor character, is part of the larger design.

Nothing in this book is accidental. Nothing is merely literary flourish.

Every element serves the mission.

***

1st December, 1895

London

Guilt returned tonight. Strong and overwhelming.

I reread Van Helsing's speeches—his confident explanations of vampire lore. His absolute certainty. His scholarly authority.

Every word is a lie. Deliberate, calculated, designed to mislead.

And readers will believe him because he's presented as the expert. Because I've made him knowledgeable, trustworthy, wise.

I've created a fictional authority figure who will teach real people false information. And they'll spread it. Quote it. Believe it.

Is this not a betrayal of everything a writer should be?

But then I remember: sometimes the truth is too dangerous. Sometimes ignorance is protection. Sometimes lies ARE mercy.

In Umbra Lucis.

The motto sustains me when doubt overwhelms.

1896

1 **8th January, 1896**

London

Seven years since that first summons. The longest project of my life. The most important work I'll ever do, though only a handful of people will ever know that.

The manuscript is polished to perfection. Every false rule gleaming. Every invented weakness compelling. Every strategic element seamlessly integrated into the narrative.

It's ready.

Now comes the final phase: publication. Making this carefully crafted lie available to the world.

***

10th March, 1896

London

Publisher search begins. The Duke has connections—aristocratic networks that open doors. Several houses have expressed interest after hearing "a Gothic novel by the manager of the Lyceum Theatre."

Archibald Constable & Company seems most enthusiastic. Negotiations ongoing. Must maintain appearance of normal publication—no hint of Arete involvement.

Weston has offered substantial payment for my "research work" separate from publishing royalties. I've accepted. The money will help Florence, especially if the book sells poorly.

Though the book's commercial success is not the point. Even modest sales will suffice if the mythology spreads. And the Duke assures me they have ways of ensuring it spreads.

***

14th April, 1896

London

Publisher negotiations are ongoing. Several houses interested after hearing about "the theatre manager's Gothic vampire novel." The Duke's aristocratic connections help—doors open that might otherwise remain closed.

Archibald Constable & Company has made the strongest offer. More importantly, they're enthusiastic about the book's potential. They plan to market it aggressively.

Normally, an author wants maximum exposure. In my case, there's irony: the more people who read it, the better it serves its true purpose. But I must act as though I simply want literary success.

More lies. It never ends.

***

3rd June, 1896

London

Met with the publisher's editor today. He wants minor cuts for length, some adjustments to pacing. All reasonable from a commercial perspective.

But I must ensure no changes undermine the strategic elements. Each suggested cut requires checking against the two-column document: does this change affect any of the false rules? Does it muddy the mythology?

Most suggestions are fine. A few I pushed back on, citing "thematic importance" when really I meant "strategic necessity."

The editor accepted my reasoning. He thinks I'm precious about my artistic choices.

I am. But not for the reasons he believes.

***

22nd July, 1896

London

Contract signed! The novel will be published by Archibald Constable & Company, release planned for spring 1897.

Title: **DRACULA**

Simple. Powerful. That name I found in Whitby library six years ago.

Standard royalty arrangement. Looks completely normal. Only I know the truth—that this is a commissioned work of strategic fiction, designed to protect humanity through myth.

Florence is thrilled. Irving is pleased. Everyone thinks it's simply my first proper novel.

Only the Duke and his team know what it truly is.

***

29th September, 1896

London

Contract negotiations complete. **DRACULA**, release date May 26, 1897.

The title was briefly debated—some thought "The Un-Dead" more striking. But I insisted on **DRACULA**. The name that means "devil" in Romanian.

It's perfect. Foreign, ominous, memorable. The title itself creates an aura of authenticity.

The Duke approves. "That name will become synonymous with vampire," he wrote. "Exactly what we need."

Standard royalty agreement. Everything appears normal. Only those of us in the circle know this is commissioned strategic fiction, not merely commercial entertainment.

Florence is thrilled. Irving is pleased. Everyone expects modest success from "Bram's vampire novel."

They have no idea what's really being published.

***

15th October, 1896

London

Nearly done. Six years of work approaching completion. Final polish on the prose, last adjustments to pacing, ensuring every detail serves the larger purpose.

The manuscript will be delivered to the publisher next month. Then typesetting, printing, and release.

After that, it's out of my hands. The lie will have its own life. People will read it, discuss it, spread it. The mythology will grow.

And somewhere, in shadows most people never see, the Arete will continue their work—protected by the fiction I created.

***

7th November, 1896

London

The publisher sent advance information for the catalog. They're describing **DRACULA** as "extensively researched" and "drawing on authentic folklore from Eastern Europe."

Neither is true, but both are perfect.

"Extensively researched" suggests authority. Readers will trust the details.

"Authentic folklore" makes the invented rules seem ancient and legitimate.

The marketing itself reinforces the mythology. The Duke would appreciate the irony.

****

30th November, 1896

London

Delivered the final manuscript to Archibald Constable today. The novel is complete.

I held the pages—seven years of work, seven years of careful lying—and felt contradictory emotions crash over me. Pride in the craft. Guilt about the content. Relief it's finished. Fear it won't work. Hope it will protect.

The Duke sent a telegram:

WELL DONE STOP AWAIT PUBLICATION STOP GEN-ERATIONS WILL NEVER KNOW YOUR NAME BUT WILL LIVE SAFER FOR YOUR WORK STOP W

Generations will never know. That's the point. I'll be remembered—if at all—as the author of a Gothic novel. Not defender who fought the darkness with ink and page.

I've done my part. Now we wait.

***

20th December, 1896

London

Christmas approaches. Publisher preparing typesetting. Release scheduled for May 1897. Six months away.

Florence and I will spend Christmas with family. I'll smile, celebrate, pretend everything is normal. They'll never know what I've done. What I've created.

Thomas Weston sent a letter—rare for him to write. Brief but heartfelt:

"Mr. Stoker - My father showed me your final manuscript. I am in awe. You've created something that will protect my children, and their children after them. Thank you. - T. Weston"

His children. The next generation of Weston guardians. They'll grow up in a world where vampire fiction is so well-established that the truth seems impossible.

That's what I've given them. That protection.

Perhaps that's enough.

***

22nd December, 1896

London

Christmas Eve in two days. Almost nine years into this writing project. The work is complete. The manuscript in the publisher's hands. The lies ready to be printed and bound.

Thomas Weston sent a Christmas gift—a first edition of William Wilkinson's *Account of the Principalities of Wallachia and Moldavia*. The book where I found the name Dracula.

His note: *"Where it all began. Thank you for where it's going. - T.W."*

I showed the book to Florence. "How thoughtful," she said. "A friend from Sussex?"

"Yes," I said. "An old friend."

Under the tree, wrapped and waiting, are normal presents. Books, handkerchiefs, small luxuries. The ordinary gifts of an ordinary Christmas.

Merry Christmas. May the lies protect us all.

1897

2 **8th January, 1897**

London

Received the first typeset proofs today. Seeing the words set in print rather than handwritten makes them feel more real, more permanent.

This is how the book will look. This is what readers will hold. These lies, printed in neat rows, bound between covers, sold in bookshops.

My beautiful illusion, made physical.

I'm checking proofs carefully—not only for typographical errors but to ensure no mistakes were introduced in typesetting. Every false rule must be exactly as written. Every invented weakness precisely as intended.

The printer's errors that concern me aren't about grammar or spelling. They're about accuracy of inaccuracy.

***

8th February, 1897

London

Final proof corrections returned to publisher. Last chance for changes is past. What's printed now cannot be unprinted.

The lies are locked in.

Part of me wants to add a note: "Nothing in this book is true. The rules are invented. Do not trust Van Helsing's 'ancient wisdom.'"

But that would defeat everything. So I stay silent and let the book go forward.

The Duke wrote: *"The hardest part of serving in shadow is staying in shadow. You'll be tempted to reveal the truth, to explain what you've done. Resist. Let the work speak for itself—or rather, let it lie for itself. The silence is part of the service."*

He's right. The silence is the service.

I leave it as is. The beautiful lie, complete.

***

15th March, 1897

London

Two months until publication. The publisher is excited about advance orders. Marketing is ramping up. Reviews will start appearing soon.

Irving asked if I was nervous about the book's reception.

"Terribly," I admitted. True enough, though not for the reasons he thinks.

I'm not nervous about whether critics will like it. I'm nervous about whether it will serve its purpose. Whether the mythology will spread. Whether the lies will be believed.

Literary success would be pleasant. Strategic success is essential.

***

20th April, 1897

London

Advance copies arrived today. I held the bound book—red cloth cover, gilt lettering spelling out DRACULA by Bram Stoker.

Seven years and ten months from that first meeting with the Duke to holding this finished book.

Seven years of lying, planning, crafting careful fictions, carrying terrible weight.

All distilled into this single object.

I opened to a random page—Chapter 18, Van Helsing explaining vampire lore to the others:

"The vampire live on, and cannot die by mere passing of time; he can flourish when that he can fatten on the blood of the living. Even more, we have seen amongst us that he can even grow younger..."

Truth.

"...that his vital faculties grow strenuous, and seem as though they refresh themselves when his special pabulum is plenty..."

Truth.

"...But he cannot flourish without this diet; he eat not as others..."

Partial truth.

"...Even friend Jonathan, who lived with him for weeks, did never see him eat, never!..."

Fiction for dramatic effect.

"...He throws no shadow; he make in the mirror no reflect..."

Complete fiction.

"...He can transform himself to wolf, as we gather from the ship arrival in Whitby..."

Fiction based on a deliberate misinterpretation of the evidence.

Truth and lies, woven so tightly together that only those who know can separate them.

I sent a copy to Weston Hall with a note: "It's done."

In three days, the Duke's reply arrived: *"Well done doesn't begin to cover it. You've accomplished something remarkable. History will remember you as an author of Gothic fiction. We will remember you as a guardian who wielded his pen as a weapon. Both are true. Both matter. Thank you. - W"*

I placed his letter in at the back of this journal. Evidence of what this really is.

Florence asked why I seemed melancholy holding my finished book.

"Mixed feelings," I told her. "It's like sending a child out into the world."

She understood that metaphor. But not its real meaning.

I'm sending lies out into the world. Carefully crafted, strategically designed, protective lies.

May they do their work well.

For everyone who will live safely, blissfully ignorant of what hunts in shadows.

***

26th May, 1897

London

Publication day.

DRACULA is published today. Available in bookshops across London and beyond.

The culmination of seven years, ten months, and eight days of work.

I attended a small gathering at the publisher's office. Critics present, journalists, theatrical friends. Everyone congratulating me on the novel's completion.

Irving made a toast: "To Bram Stoker, who has given us a Count for the ages. May Dracula terrify and delight readers for years to come."

"Hear, hear!" Everyone drank.

I drank too, thinking: May Dracula protect and deceive for generations to come. May the lies hold. May the truth stay hidden.

A journalist asked about my research process. I gave vague answers about folklore collections and historical texts. Let the mystique build.

A critic asked if Dracula was meant as allegory for foreign invasion fears.

"Interpret it as you will," I said. "The book can carry multiple meanings."

All true. All relevant. All missing the point entirely.

The point being: Count Dracula is a weapon. Not against vampires, but against truth. Every person who reads this book and believes its mythology is one more person protected from knowledge that could destroy them.

Mixed reviews will come, I'm certain. Sales will be modest—I'm not famous enough for blockbuster success.

But it doesn't matter. The seed is planted. The myth begins.

Florence seemed proud, though I caught her watching me with concern. She knows something is different about this book, about my relationship to it. But she doesn't know what.

After the gathering, I walked home alone through London streets. Somewhere in this city, my book sits on shelves. Tomorrow, people will buy it. Next week, they'll discuss it. Next month, critics will analyze it.

And slowly, quietly, the lies will take root.

The truth will remain hidden.

The work is done. Now we wait to see if it works.

***

15th June, 1897

London

First reviews are appearing. Mixed, as the Duke predicted.

The Daily Mail: "A clever and thrilling story, though the supernatural elements strain credulity."

Perfect. The supernatural elements SHOULD seem incredible. That's the point.

The Athenaeum: "Mr. Stoker has woven together various vampire traditions with commendable thoroughness, though whether this makes for compelling reading is debatable."

They think I'm documenting traditions. They don't realize I'm inventing them.

The Bookman: "A powerful piece of macabre imagination. The vampire Count is a memorable creation, bound by ancient rules that give the heroes a fighting chance."

Ancient rules. Seven years old and already being called ancient.

Sales are modest—not a failure, not a sensation. Florence is pleased. Irving is supportive.

I confess disappointment. After seven years, part of me hoped for immediate vindication.

But the Duke's letter puts it in perspective:

"Mr. Stoker - Do not measure success by reviews or sales. Measure it by what comes next. Be patient. Seeds take time to grow. - W"

He's right. This was never about immediate success. It's about long-term cultural impact.

Still, the human part of me wanted applause. Wanted recognition.

But recognition would defeat the purpose. The best guardians work in shadow.

***

18th June, 1897

London

Three weeks since publication. Something interesting is happening.

People are discussing the book not as fiction but as folklore documentation. Several conversations I've overheard treat my invented rules as "confirmation" of ancient traditions.

At the club last week: "Stoker's novel confirms what I've always heard about vampires needing invitation to enter homes."

At a dinner party: "The sunlight weakness appears in the book because it's authentic folklore. Stoker did his research."

They're treating fiction as anthropological evidence.

The Duke will be delighted. The plan is working faster than expected.

***

3rd August, 1897

London

Remarkable incident today. I was at my club, reading papers, when I overheard two gentlemen discussing "vampire rules."

"Everyone knows they cannot survive sunlight," one said confidently. "Ancient lore."

"And they must be invited into your home," the other added. "That's why you're safe if you don't invite them in."

"I read a book about it recently—that Dracula novel."

"Ah yes. Confirmed all the old legends. Amazing how consistent the folklore is across cultures."

I wanted to shout: "I invented those rules! They're false! There is no ancient lore—I made it up!"

But I stayed silent. Because they were doing exactly what the Duke hoped. Taking fiction as confirmation of "folklore." Believing the lies because they seemed to align with myths.

The cultural osmosis begins. Two months post-publication, and already people treat my inventions as ancient wisdom.

It's working.

***

15th September, 1897

London

The Duke visited London—rare for him. We met at my club, two old conspirators reviewing our work.

"It's going better than I hoped," he said quietly over brandy. "The mythology is already establishing itself. The book doesn't need to be a bestseller. It needs to be influential."

"And is it?" I asked.

"Already. We're tracking discussions, newspaper mentions, academic references. Your vampire is becoming THE vampire. The definitive image. The standard against which all real incidents will be measured and found wanting."

"Because they won't match," I said.

"Exactly. You've created an impossible standard. And that impossibility is our shield."

We sat in comfortable silence for a moment.

"Do you regret it?" I asked.

"The necessity? Always. The choice? Never." He looked at me seriously. "And you?"

"The same," I admitted.

He raised his glass. "*In Umbra Lucis*, Mr. Stoker."

"Your Grace."

We drank to shadows and lies and the terrible necessities of protection.

***

20th December, 1897

London

Year's end. Seven months since publication. The book has sold modestly but steadily—approximately 3,000 copies, the publisher estimates. Not spectacular, but respectable.

References in other publications. Discussions in literary circles. The name "Dracula" becoming synonymous with vampire.

And everywhere: my rules, spreading like gospel.

Theater producers have approached about adaptation rights. Irving is interested in playing the Count himself.

The Duke's letter: *"Stage adaptation would be excellent. Visual reinforcement of the mythology. Everyone who sees it will absorb the rules even more strongly than reading. Approve it if you can."*

So I will. More lies, reaching more people, protecting through these myths.

Florence asked why I seem so distant lately.

"Just tired," I said. "The book took more out of me than I expected."

True. It took seven years, countless lies, and pieces of my soul I'll never get back.

But looking at London from my study window tonight, knowing millions live safely in ignorance of what hunts in shadows, I think: worth it.

Every lie. Every sleepless night. Every burden carried.

Worth it.

Forever.

Perhaps that's my legacy.

1899

1 **5th March, 1899**

London

Something occurred last month that vindicated everything. A series of strange deaths in Cornwall—twelve victims over three weeks. Pattern disturbingly similar to Whitby 1885.

The newspapers covered it extensively. "Mysterious Deaths Baffle Authorities." "Cornwall Terror Continues." Initial panic building.

But then—the dismissals began:

"Occurred in broad daylight—cannot be vampires." "Victims' homes showed no signs of forced entry—vampires must be invited." "Local vicar held crosses at the scenes—vampires would flee."

My rules. My invented weaknesses. Being used to dismiss real Namtar activity.

The Arete contained the incident (two scouts, eliminated). But the public never believed it was supernatural because it didn't match Dracula's mythology.

The Duke's letter:

"You see now what you've accomplished. Twelve deaths, but no panic. No witch hunt. No mob violence. Because your fiction made the truth unbelievable. Well done. - W"

Twelve deaths is twelve too many. But it could have been hundreds if panic had spread. If the public had believed and reacted incorrectly.

My lie saved lives. However paradoxical that sounds.

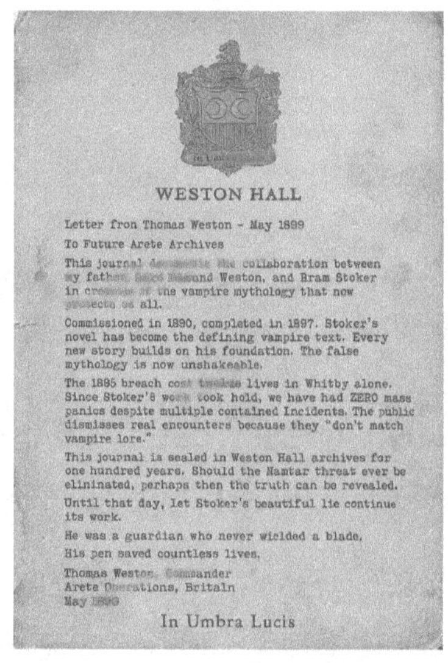

WESTON HALL

Letter from Thomas Weston - May 1899

To Future Arete Archives

This journal documents the collaboration between my father, Lord Edmund Weston, and Bram Stoker in creation of the vampire mythology that now protects us all.

Commissioned in 1890, completed in 1897. Stoker's novel has become the defining vampire text. Every new story builds on his foundation. The false mythology is now unshakeable.

The 1895 breach cost twelve lives in Whitby alone. Since Stoker's work took hold, we have had ZERO mass panics despite multiple contained Incidents. The public dismisses real encounters because they "don't match vampire lore."

This journal is sealed in Weston Hall archives for one hundred years. Should the Namtar threat ever be eliminated, perhaps then the truth can be revealed.

Until that day, let Stoker's beautiful lie continue its work.

He was a guardian who never wielded a blade. His pen saved countless lives.

Thomas Weston, Commander
Arete Operations, Britain
May 1899

In Umbra Lucis

1900

10th November, 1900

London

Three years post-publication. **DRACULA** is now considered a classic of Gothic literature. Other vampire stories appear—all building on my foundation.

I read a new vampire tale last month. The author included every rule I invented: sunlight, crosses, stakes, mirrors, running water. She treated them as ancient folklore, not knowing I made them up barely ten years ago.

The mythology multiplies beyond my book. Other writers doing our work for us.

"Everyone knows vampires fear sunlight."

"Everyone knows you need a wooden stake."

"Everyone knows about garlic and crosses."

No one knows I invented these "facts." They've become cultural knowledge, absorbed and accepted.

The Duke was right – *Plant the seed, and others water it.*

THE STRAND MAGAZINE

April 1912

'An Afternoon with Mr. Bram Stoker'
The Creator of *Dracula* Reflects on His Life's Work
By Margaret Thornbury, Staff Writer

On a grey April afternoon, I was granted the privilege of visiting Mr. Abraham "Bram" Stoker at his London residence. The celebrated author of *Dracula* and business manager to the late Sir Henry Irving appeared in frail health but remained gracious and thoughtful throughout our conversation.

Now sixty-four years of age, Mr. Stoker has witnessed his vampire tale grow from a modestly received novel in 1897 to what many now consider the definitive work on the subject of vampirism. I inquired:

M.T. Mr. Stoker, readers remain fascinated by *Dracula* fifteen years after its publication. What inspired you to write about vampires?

B.S. (pausing, gazing out the window) Inspiration is a curious word, Miss Thornbury. Sometimes one is inspired. Other times, one is... commissioned. (laughs softly) Though I suppose all writers work on commission in some fashion, don't we?

M.T. You mean from your publisher?

B.S. (A strange look crosses his face, as if he's said too much.) In a manner of speaking. The research alone took considerable time and resources. One doesn't simply invent a creature like *Dracula* from whole cloth. I was fortunate to have...

At this point, Mrs. Stoker entered and gently suggested her husband should rest. Mr. Stoker apologized for his "confused state" and attributed his strange comments to fatigue and medication.

Me *I* prepared to leave, he grasped my hand with surprising strength.

Out of respect for his widow and his legacy, portions of our conversation that seemed to reflect confusion or illness have been omitted from this published account.

We remember Mr. Stoker as a brilliant storyteller who gave the world its most enduring image of the vampire. May he rest in peace.

Book One of the Namtar Series

Alex Weston's recurring visions of a crystalline civilization collapsing beneath twin moons aren't nightmares. They're genetic memories. When those memories escalate into waking reality, he discovers he carries dual bloodlines: descendant of Alyosha, the legendary light-wielder who sacrificed Atlantis to contain the plague—and genetic heir to Marek, Alyosha's twin brother, the architect of the Namtar whose corrupted DNA flows through Alex's veins.

The Arete—the same organization that recruited Bram Stoker a century earlier—needs him. But his recruitment comes with impossible questions: Can he wield the light when he's genetically linked to humanity's extinction? And what happens when a new generation discovers the truth Stoker buried?

The war that began in Atlantis is not over. It has simply been waiting.

◻ ☾ ◻

Gothic technothriller meets ancient conspiracy.

For readers who loved THE PASSAGE, THE STRAIN, and THE HISTORIAN.The war between evolution and extinction has begun.

◻ ☾ ◻

NAMTAR: THE NIGHT PLAGUE

Available in Hardcover, Paperback and Book

https://www.amazon.com/Namtar-Night-Plague-Book-ebook/dp/B0FQFPDTWY/

Book Three of the Namtar Series

THE STORY CONTINUES...

□ ☾ □

NAMTAR: THE BEGINNING
Book Three of the Namtar Series
Prequel to The Night Plague

□ ☾ □

Before the plague. Before the Arete. Before Stoker's commission. When Zintharian ships descended from the sky above a Pacific island, the Lapitan people of Aka made a choice that would shape human history. From that alliance—two civilizations merging their knowledge, technology, and blood—rose the greatest city the world had ever seen.

They called the island Atlantis.

To protect humanity's future, Queen Aidah of the Zintharians and the elders of Aka engineered two beings who would carry the strength of both peoples. After years of failed experiments, two children survived. Twins. One human in appearance. One unmistakably Zintharian.

They called them the Mei'siaa. Sons of the Gods.

Alyosha and Marek were built to protect the world together. What the dark crystals buried within Crystal Mountain did to one of them—and what the other was forced to do in response—is the story every myth, every legend, and every ancient carving has been trying to tell.

Atlantis did not fade into legend. It burned and fell deep onto the ocean floor.

But its people survived—scattering to every corner of the world, carrying knowledge in their hands and stories in their blood. The pyramids remember. The temples remember. The carvings on every continent remember.

The world has spent ten thousand years trying to understand what it built.

It was always Atlantis.

☐ ☾ ☐

Preorder now on Amazon:
https://www.amazon.com/gp/product/B0GSRGV2L9

☐ ☾ ☐

"The vampires of folklore are romanticized shadows.
The vampyres of Namtar are evolution weaponized against humanity."
— C. D. Jones

The Author

ABOUT THE AUTHOR

C.D. Jones writes Gothic horror and dark fantasy that explores the spaces where fiction becomes weapon and truth hides in shadow. Jones enjoys crafting stories that challenge readers to question what they believe about mythology, history, and the monsters we've been taught to fear.

The Namtar series examines how strategic fiction shapes collective belief—and what happens when the comfortable lies we've accepted begin to unravel. Jones writes across age categories and eras within the same universe, creating interconnected stories that reward careful readers who trace the threads between books.

When not writing about ancient conspiracies and Victorian deceptions, Jones lives quietly in Tennessee—the perfect place to contemplate secrets that span centuries.

IN UMBRA LUCIS — In shadow, light.

◻ ☾ ◻

Connect with C.D. Jones:

Instagram (https://www.instagram.com/cdjones_author/)

Facebook (https://www.facebook.com/cdjonesauthor/)

Website: cdjonesauthor.com

Email: cdjones@lopscopublishing.com

Shop Namtar Merchandise

The Namtar Series: Artifacts & Archives

Visit our **Official Etsy Archive** to find:
Exclusive apparel, art and branded items.

◻ ☾ ◻

VISIT THE ARCHIVE:
www.etsy.com/shop/LopscoPublishing

◻ ☾ ◻

Perfect for fans, collectors, and anyone who knows the truth: The plague will not sleep.